Kismet

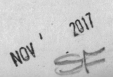

Kismet

Raynesha Pittman

www.urbanbooks.net

Urban Books, LLC
300 Farmingdale Road, NY-Route 109
Farmingdale, NY 11735

ISBN 13: 978-1-62286-894-0
ISBN 10: 1-62286-894-3

First Mass Market Printing April 2017
Printed in the United States of America

10 9 8 7 6 5 4 3 2 1

This is a work of fiction. Any references or similarities to actual events, real people, living or dead, or to real locales are intended to give the novel a sense of reality. Any similarity in other names, characters, places, and incidents is entirely coincidental.

Distributed by Kensington Publishing Corp.
Submit orders to:
Customer Service
400 Hahn Road
Westminster, MD 21157-4627
Phone: 1-800-733-3000
Fax: 1-800-659-2436

Kismet

by

Raynesha Pittman

Chapter 1

Don't Call Tyrone!

I should wake Tyrone's sorry ass up. For the last two months, he's been talking shit about what he would do to me if I gave him a chance. Three and a half minutes after that "chance," he rolled over and went to sleep. I'm so tired of these extralarge, Magnum-wearing, five-good-strokes-giving niggas always bragging about their dicks like they're the cure for cancer or the solution to world peace. I haven't witnessed a dick do anything but get hard and nut.

Men seem to think that if they have made one woman scream their names or come, they can do it to every woman they sleep with. The truth is that most of us fake it so we won't hurt their egos. The male ego is complicated and, in some inexplicable way, it's connected to their dicks, which I'll never understand.

Don't twist my words. I love dick and have screamed out many names in pleasure. What I'm saying is this: Different strokes for different folks. What worked for Jan might not work for Jane, so don't be mad when I say it isn't good. You can't use the same strokes on me that you use with every other woman you've been with and think I can't detect how you have mastered the position.

If you insist on stroking me with your routine stroke, you got the wrong woman. I'm twenty-nine years old. I couldn't give a damn about a man's ego. I want to be satisfied, and prerehearsed moves aren't going to get it. If he isn't capable of satisfying me with the natural flow of the mood we are in, he doesn't deserve to spend another second inside me.

When I was younger, I would do all that fake moaning and back scratching. Hell, I was the best orgasm faker in the world . . . until it hit me that he was truly enjoying it and I was better off masturbating. Those days are over. I have a thirty-second rule now. If I haven't gotten wetter, started shaking to where I can't control it, or had the urge to pull him in deeper within the first thirty seconds, he has to get the fuck off me. The only flaw I've found with this rule is that there are no warning signs if he's a two-minute man. That's how Tyrone got away with three-and-a half-minutes.

Yes, I'm mad about it because I could have been under, or on top of, somebody else tonight. Everything in me told me not to fuck Tyrone, but my pussy has a mind of her own, so I let her have her way and went ahead and slept with Keisha's baby daddy. Listening to Keisha's broke, food stamp-selling ass brag about sex with her son's father was one of the reasons I wanted to fuck him in the first place.

I wanted to see if he was really as good as she had said. "Tyrone does this" and "Tyrone does that." She promoted his dick like Don King would promote a Tyson fight.

I believed her since Tyrone had the math of a man that could handle his business in bed. He was six foot one and 195 pounds of pure muscle, black as midnight, bowlegged without the handicapped walk most bowlegged men have, and well-groomed for a man who never left the hood.

Most don't have time to hit a barbershop every two weeks, but Tyrone did. He kept the old, Steve Harvey perfect edge up with more waves in his hair than the ocean. He possessed deep dimples that complemented his face, leading to a sexy, perfect, white smile, surrounded by LL Cool J "Doing It Well"-era lips.

Tyrone was always in a new white, Pro Club T-shirt, rocking the newest pair of Jordans or classic high-top Chuck Taylors with fat laces. His way of dressing would look broke and immature to me on any other man, but on him, it was mouthwatering.

What I found to be most sexy about him was when he was on the basketball court in his wife beater, sweating hard and panting heavily from smoking too much weed while trying to talk shit after losing.

How does that add up to being able to handle his business in bed? Do the math. Basketball has four quarters, and he never used a substitute, which equals stamina. He talked shit whenever he was losing or had lost, which meant he had a winning mind frame. How many men you know want to lose in the bed? My point exactly. That shoe-size myth most women judge men by meant nothing to me. I've slept with a lot of size twelve- and thirteen-inch feet and learned that they don't do shit but untuck the sheets at the foot of the bed. It must be embarrassing when your shoe size is twice the size of your condom filler.

Keisha had made Tyrone out to be a dark chocolate, boxer-wearing Superman, whose superpower was his ten-inch long, two-inch wide dick. Looks like my pussy was kryptonite because I ended up with a no-stamina-having Clark Kent. Nothing about those three minutes was super.

Guess my math was wrong. I forgot to subtract the fact that my pussy is platinum compared to the miles Keisha has on hers. I could slap that heifer for lying to me like that. What Keisha failed to realize about me is that I haven't considered her a friend since high school, which led to my final reason for giving Tyrone some. That slut slept with my first boyfriend, Kevin, and took his virginity while we were dating. She convinced him that I would never give it up, so he had sex with her at his father's house while his dad was at work. Payback was coming. I just didn't think it would take that long to get it. We were kids when it happened, and I might be wrong in some people's eyes, but I don't give a damn. Each ho has her day, and for Keisha, today was that day.

Something about the thought of sex and revenge made me want Tyrone even more. I am not the only woman on this earth who has used sex to get revenge, and I won't be the last to use it either. When our man cheats on us, what do we do? We go sleep with somebody too. Even men use sex for revenge. What do they do when we don't pay them enough attention, but our so-called friend does? They have sex with her, and, when we find out they slept with her, the first reason they give is, "She was there for me when you wasn't." That's a form of revenge for not putting him first. Let's not pretend that sex and revenge haven't gone hand in hand.

This ho, Keisha, was known for sexing everybody's man. She didn't need revenge to give your man some. She did it because she wanted to sample something new, like wine tasting. All the guys around our way wanted to sample her too. Her mother was Mexican, and her father was black, so she had bright yellow skin, light brown eyes, hair that fell to the middle of her back, and no ass at all. But she had double-D breasts, and she spoke English and Spanish fluently, so once she reached thirteen years old, she became the girl every guy wanted, and it seemed she wanted every guy.

If you had a working dick, you were Keisha's type. The sad part about it is she was in love with Tyrone. But, like the saying goes, "You can't make a ho a housewife." Due to Keisha's ho status in my old neighborhood, she couldn't expect anything more than an occasional quickie from her son's father.

I can't stand Keisha or her two homegirls, Christina and Melinda. I've slept with their baby daddies too, but they had more to offer me than Tyrone. At least they paid a bill or wined and dined me. Tyrone's ass was broke with all that small-time dope dealing, and his neighborhood rap career wasn't shit. Where I grew up, everybody raps and hustles. There wasn't a big-time dope dealer in our area because there were about fifty small-time ones who shared customers, and all fifty of them had gotten a piece of Keisha.

Keisha hooked up with Tyrone after I went off to college, so I don't know all the details of their past relationship. From what Tyrone told me, they hooked up after a barbeque, had sex in the backseat of his Caprice, and three months later, she told him she was pregnant. Seven months later, DNA proved little TJ was his. Keisha had reached a hood rat's dream. She was given food stamps, medical, dental, Section 8, and child support. Now that's just his side of the story.

Too bad Tyrone doesn't have a real job to actually pay child support. He could have been somebody worth having a baby by if he wouldn't have fucked himself up. Tyrone had a full basketball scholarship to USC. He lost it when he decided to drive around in his car while his so-called friends did drive-bys. He was arrested and given the most time because he was the oldest, and it was his car. Tyrone didn't pull the trigger, but that didn't mean anything to the university. They snatched up their offer without listening to his side of the story.

The youngest guy in the car, Will, was also sentenced. He was sent to a juvenile correction center for a few years while he fought his case. After two years of fighting, he was sentenced to camp, where he got his mind right and got on his feet. When Will came home, he got his juvenile record sealed and went to a junior college where he took up criminal justice. He now works downtown at the criminal courts building as a sheriff.

I wish there was a fairy-tale ending for Tyrone, but he got caught up in the thug life and started selling drugs. He had the chance to close his record and get back on the right foot, but selling all that small-time dope got him arrested one too many times. In my opinion, it's never too late to get yourself together. You have to want it like Will did. I wonder if Will's sexy ass is still single. I have to make sure I put him on my things-to-do list next week if he still is.

I got out of the bed to go lock myself in my bathroom with Big Jamal, my faithful vibrator, to finish up the job since the thought of Will's sexy, ex-football-playing ass had gotten me back wet. It hit me that this waste of a condom is at my hideaway spot and his sorry ass drove here. I could, therefore, kick him out and go home to get ready for my workweek.

"Tyrone, wake up," I said, sounding as nice as I could because he had drooled all over my satin sheets and didn't deserve—or earn—the right to go to sleep in the first place.

"Tyrone, I need you to leave . . . now. I just remembered that I need to finish up my reports for work on Monday. So I need to head home, boo."

He rolled over with that sexy-ass smile and said, "Come here, beautiful, and let me eat that pussy before I go."

I had to bite my tongue to keep myself from screaming out, "Hell, no," but, once again, I let my pussy call the shots, and then flew on my back.

"Okay, Tyrone, but that's it. Then we have to go." He agreed.

Besides my thirty-second rule, I have a head rule. Never turn down an offer to receive head unless they needed visible dental work, had rotten breath, or a tongue ring. A lot of people don't take time to sanitize their mouth jewelry, and I don't want whatever bacteria that are living on it swimming around in me.

Men don't ever turn down head and will quickly tell you to suck it. They say, "Suck my dick" to everything. When you're arguing, "Suck my . . .," when you're trying to put them in the mood . . . "Baby, just suck it; it will get hard," so, why can't we do the same? I know it isn't "lady-like" to walk around saying, "Lick me" or "Eat me," but it should be an unspoken requirement.

He dragged me to the edge of the bed by my hips, spread my legs apart, and started at my ankles, sucking and licking me slowly. He seemed to know what he was doing. He made his way down to the folds of my legs, nibbling softly and licking his own lips to put on a show for me since I was watching. My pussy jumped, and I was instantly ready to feel his tongue on my pearl. He gripped my butt with his left hand and said softly, "Grab the back of my head, baby, and show me where you want me to put my mouth."

As if I was scared he would withdraw his request, I grabbed the back of his head, just a few inches above his neck, closed my eyes, and led him to the lips that protected my pearl. He kissed up and down my lips, then, using his tongue to separate them, he made it to my pearl tongue. That's when I confirmed Tyrone wasn't shit.

He couldn't even do the simple task of giving me head correctly. He kept coming up for air like he was drowning. I know I'm known for soaking through a mattress or two, but I didn't know I needed to supply niggas with life jackets.

"Hell, no!" I heard the words come out of my mouth and at this point, I wasn't going to stop them. "What the hell was that, Tyrone? How in the fuck did you expect me to find pleasure in that shit?" I was waiting on an answer.

Instead, he snapped, "What the hell you mean, you uppity-ass bitch? You have been complaining since we hooked up earlier. First, the damn food at your favorite, expensive restaurant didn't taste right 'cause your favorite cook wasn't there. I tried to be nice to your petty ass and pay for that expensive shit and never heard the words 'thank you' come outta your mouth. What did your too-good-for-the-hood ass do next? Oh yeah, you made me drive an hour and thirty minutes from LA to meet you up here on the Pacific Coast Highway 'cause you like to see the ocean while you're getting fucked, instead of paying sixty-five dollars and going to the Snooty Fox on Western like I had planned. Fuck your college degrees and your good-ass job. You're still Na-Na to me, the little tomboy with the

jumper from the park, and if you weren't fucking all them bitches on the down low, you
would know a good man when you saw one,
you dyke bitch."

See, the old me would have flipped over the
bed and tried to fight him. That person died
when I moved out of South Central, LA. Instead,
I thought I'd give him a piece of what he gave me.

"First off, quick draw, the fastest nut shooter
from the west, my name is Savannah, and it's
called a *chef* not a *cook*. Second, I was born on
the East Side. That doesn't restrict me to do what
East Siders do. I don't have sex on ten-dollar an
hour sheets, Mr. Small-Time Trapper six years
in a row. I know where I'm from, and I'll be dead
or dying before I go back there to live, so get
your tired ass out of my $600 a night time-share
air and hit the 10 freeway back to your EBT-card
atmosphere. Do you need gas money? Or did
your probation officer give you gate money when
you got released? Your mouth still smells like
an inmate named Big 'D,' so don't question my
sexuality until you get yours in check."

At that moment, Tyrone jumped out of bed,
threw his clothes on, grabbed his keys, said his
last, "Fuck you, bitch," and left.

Chapter 2

Can I Tell My Story

On the ride back to Malibu, which was only twenty minutes away from my rental property, I kept replaying what Tyrone had said to me over and over again.

"You're still Na-Na to me, the little tomboy with the jumper from the park."

It wasn't the anger in his words that was bugging me, but the fact he called and still saw me as Na-Na, the little girl who should have been a boy because of her basketball skills. I have worked hard to be the opposite of that little girl, and he was too blind to see it. His broke-ass opinion really didn't mean anything to me. It's just that those were the people who needed to see my change the most. I lost all the chubbiness I had as a child and am now 165 pounds of pure thickness. My waist is a size 10. Due to having toned thighs and hips, I wear a size 12. Besides the $5,700 I spent turning my A-cups to DDs, I am all natural.

I'm five foot seven with a peanut butter complexion, and my eyes are slanted like I have Asian heritage. I used to wear a 1990s Toni Braxton short haircut, but I grew it out to a shoulder-length, layered cut. I get a manicure and a pedicure once a week so my feet and hands could be as soft as my butt. I'm not a swap meet or flea market shopper. I only place designer clothes on this body. I don't mean hip-hop designers like Fetish or Ecko Red. I'm talking about Armani and Dolce suits. I relax in DKNY. I do own a few Apple Bottom, Rocawear, and Dereon items, but that is mostly to blend in when I'm around company that wears those labels. To be honest, I love House of Dereon and Baby Phat clothing, but the places I shop don't carry them, and I don't shop online because I like to try on my clothing.

How could he not see the difference? My childhood years were rough, but they made me into the successful woman that I am now. I grew up in a house with four men and my grandmother. It was my grandmother's two-bedroom house. We were very poor. We never missed a meal, but money was always funny. My father had full custody of my brother and me after he deemed my mother unfit because she would leave for weeks without notice. Daddy moved us out of her house and brought us to live with his mother.

My mother had an addiction to money, and she got it in all the "wrong ways." To this day, I still don't know what that meant, but everyone said it when speaking of her. She went to school to be a nurse of some sort and met my father while he was recovering from a car accident. Whenever he told the story of him and my mother meeting, he would smile and say, "Trisha nursed me back to health."

Trisha, a.k.a., my mother was gone before my first birthday, so I don't have any fond memories to hold on to. If I knew more about her, I would tell more, but that's all the information my daddy ever gave us about her besides she had a love for the South and lived down there for many years before she moved to California. That's why I was named Savannah, and my older brother, Memphis. My uncle, Steve, would joke with my daddy and say things like, "Trisha had to go back South to her real life" and smart shit like that. I hated the fact that he knew more about my mother than I did.

Memphis had made the mistake of asking my father if our mama was a prostitute before becoming a nurse, and that question got him slapped in the mouth. "Boy, don't you *ever* speak poorly of your mother! She is a damn good woman. There are just some things you will never understand." My mama must have told him that line, because he used it whenever people asked him, "What happen to Trisha?"

He always called my mama a good woman, but what kind of good woman leaves her two small children to be raised by their daddy while she lived her dreams? It wasn't long before I realized my mother would never come back. Whatever life she had in the South must have been better than raising her kids and being married to my daddy. I decided if I ever were to meet her, I'd kick her ass for leaving us the way she did.

I raised myself to be a woman. I didn't have a positive black woman in my life. My grand-mother was around, but she was very sick and didn't have the energy to help my daddy raise us.

I didn't get the "period talk" or the one about the "birds and the bees." I learned how to be a woman by incidents that occurred. I started my period at twelve years old. I thought I was dying, like any other girl would if no one told her she was going to bleed for five days and live to see another five days of bleeding twenty-eight days later. Lucky for me, Uncle Steve was a ladies' man and just so happened to have one of his boy toys at the house that gave me a pad and explained it to me. I could point fingers, but I don't blame anyone for the way I am. Maybe I would have turned out differently if I had a strong, positive black mother in my life, but I didn't. Why should I dwell on it?

Since our mother was still alive, my daddy didn't date. He never said it, but I think he was waiting on her to get herself together and come back, which never happened. In addition, there wasn't room in that house for another adult. My daddy's brothers, Uncle Steve and Uncle Johnny, lived with us too. Uncle Johnny was my favorite uncle when I was a child. He was a basketball coach at the park down the street, hence, my love for basketball.

At the age of eight, he started me as his point guard on his all-boys basketball team, and I kept that position or shooting guard throughout high school. My basketball talents put me on the "Do Not Date" list by the fellas, and it kept girls from being my friends because I was too boyish. They assumed I was a lesbian, and, because we were poor and I couldn't keep up with the latest fashions, I sometimes wore my brother's clothes. It did look like I wanted to be a boy.

With so many memories to block out, I remember telling my father that I would make it to the pros and we would never live poor again. He looked me dead in my eyes when he told me he couldn't afford to send me to college, whenever that time came. How in the hell can you look in your ten-year-old daughter's face and tell her she has no future? I didn't let that hold me back, and I still promised to get a full scholarship and get us out of the hood.

After hearing my dreams of being someone one day get shot down by my own father, I decided to let whatever people thought of me become my reality. I started wearing cornrows straight back, basketball shorts everywhere I went, and carrying my basketball with me like it was my lifeline. I had a goal, and I was going to reach it, even if I was the only person to believe in it. No one's thoughts of me were going to stop me, so why should I put energy into impressing them?

Hanging out with the boys on my team who accepted me landed me into kissing Kim on my sixteenth birthday. This made everyone's thoughts of me being a lesbian correct. Kim was on a rival high school basketball team and was a known lesbian, she didn't try to hide it. She had dated every lesbian or bisexual girl in her high school and in our league.

Kim invited me skating to celebrate my birthday, and since I didn't have any friends to celebrate it with, I took her up on the offer. At the end of the night on our ride back to my house, she pulled over and told me that we should hook up. Not wanting to seem like I wasn't with it, I agreed by sealing the deal with a kiss. Kissing soon became fingering, and finally, full-blown sex with hours of amazing head. If there was something I didn't know how to do sexually, Kim would teach me, and made sure I was the best at it.

I had never given head, not even to a boy before, and had no clue what I had gotten into. She showed me how to eat her using an orange to help teach her lesson. Cutting the orange into four slices, she peeled all the skin off one slice and placed it on a plate vertically. "This is the pearl tongue," she said, while she took the next unpeeled slice and laid it horizontally on the plate under the first slice.

"The top half of this piece is the skin between the pearl tongue and the entrance. The peel around the orange is the lips, and the bottom half is the entrance."

I watched her suck and lick on the pretend pearl tongue; then she licked the skin in between the pearl tongue and entrance over and over again. She stuck her tongue in the part of the orange that acted as the entrance and placed her mouth over the whole thing.

While kissing the orange peel, she said, "When you're making love to a girl you really like, don't rush it. Kiss her lips and pearl tongue first. Make her crave you."

I watched for two minutes or more, and then said, "I'm ready."

From the way Kim reacted, I knew I was a fast learner. I had her scooting away from me, saying, "You sure you ain't done this before?" That made me want to keep going, and I did. Giving her head not only turned me on, I soon began to come from it. There is something about the taste of it that turns me on. I can't explain it, but I now know why men can't live without it.

In our first year of dating, the rumors of me being a lesbian circulated around my neighborhood and got to my uncle Steve. I'll never forget that night. It was after one of my basketball games. Uncle Johnny and I sat outside on my granny's porch going over my stats like we always did.

"Look, Na-Na, if you want to get picked up by a college, you have to be a team player. Get your assist up. Nobody likes a hot dog. Those rumors of there being a professional women's league are true. I'd hate for it to pass you up because you won't pass the damn ball."

Right before I could defend my not passing the ball, Uncle Steve came out of the house, walked up to me, and grabbed me by the front of my jersey. "What the hell is wrong with you?"

Not understanding what he meant, I asked, "What are you talking about now, Uncle Steve?" He was a known liar and would go to any lengths to get someone to believe him. I think Uncle Johnny thought he was up to his old tricks again too. He grabbed Steve's hand off me, making him release my jersey.

"So, you're having sex with that dyke girl, Kim, you always with, huh?"

That was the first time I realized I was lesbian. It was also the first time I saw both of my uncles disappointed in me. I didn't answer the question. I just looked at both of them hoping they would leave it alone. My uncle Johnny told me to go in the house and shower. When I got out, everyone, including my daddy, knew about it and wanted to talk to me about it. No one in that house had ever paid any attention to me except for Uncle Johnny, yet everyone thought they could yell at me, including Memphis.

I felt the words come out of my mouth. "Look, I'm seventeen years old and will be eighteen in two months. If I want to be a lesbian, there isn't anything any of you can do about it, so deal with it."

The words came easily, but the slap across my face from my daddy made me wish I had thought about what I said before saying it.

"I won't have no lesbian for a daughter, do you hear me, Savannah?" I had gone seventeen years without him hitting me, but that night, it all changed. After twenty or more hits from his belt and everyone's show of disappointment, I promised to act like a girl, date boys, and start making friends.

It was too late for me when it came to my brother, Memphis, however. He disowned me completely and helped everyone in my neighborhood make fun of me and put me down. He even gave Keisha all the details of what happened between me and my daddy—in exchange for sex, of course. I prayed his dick would fall off. To this day, with all the changes I've made, Memphis still doesn't talk to me. I saw him when he got out of jail and at my grandmother's funeral, but he didn't look my way. Oh well, fuck him too.

My next task was to break up with Kim, and surprisingly, it was easy for me to do because I found out Kevin had a crush on me. I started dating him. I wanted to have sex with Kevin, but I wanted the fairy-tale sex where he took my virginity while the sun rose and soft music played. I knew Kevin wasn't that kind of guy, so

I decided he wasn't the one. However, I was glad he was there to help me get over Kim.

It wasn't the same for Kim. She always had girls flirting with her, so I thought she would bounce back from me breaking up with her quickly. It didn't happen that way at all. She drove past my house two and three times a day, called my phone all throughout the night, and even went as far as fouling me hard during a game, for which she was given a technical foul.

I had to lie to her to get her to leave me alone. I told her I really wanted to continue dating her, but my father had gotten involved and was monitoring everything I was doing. I asked her if we could have sex one last time and go our separate ways in a better fashion than I had done it the first time, and it worked. When that was said and done, it was time to make friends.

I went straight to Keisha because she was the most popular girl I knew. My father had heard the rumors of her sleeping around with different guys, so she wasn't on his list of potential lesbians. It was sad that my father would prefer I be a slut than a lesbian, but whatever made him happy and kept me from getting beat again . . .

Keisha, Christina, and Melinda accepted me into their crew because I provided them with someone to make fun of. They treated me like shit and talked about me to my face. I didn't let it get to me because I had received acceptance letters from eight colleges and had started counting down to the day I left.

Keisha wanted me to become a ho like her. I remember her leaving me to walk home from the skating rink because she met some guys that wanted to have sex with us, and I refused to go. The next day, she told me that I had left her to handle both of them by herself, and that I owed her big time.

I didn't even complain about my walk home. I just apologized and told her I wouldn't do it again. I knew my future didn't include her or the "Ho Squad"—the name I called them behind their backs. I had two months to go, and when I left, I wasn't taking any of them with me.

I would dream of Keisha getting AIDS and begging me for help. In my dreams, I would treat her like she was invisible and keep walking. That was evil of me to be excited about something horrible happening to her, but it made it easier to be her friend the next day. I felt like she was the shot caller in the daytime, and I was the shot caller at night, even if it was in dreamland.

If Keisha's ass would have ever caught fire, I wouldn't have spit on her. Instead, I'd barbeque ribs on her ass and have a cookout.

I didn't think Keisha could do me any worse than the way she treated me until she broke the camel's back by sleeping with Kevin. That was the final straw.

Everybody knew about it too and expected me to fight her over it. I wasn't scared, but what would I look like fighting her over some dick I had already decided I didn't want?

Keisha even assumed I was going to beat her up. She invited me to her house and asked if we were still cool. I played the role and said, "Yes." It took everything in me not to knock her teeth down her throat.

Keisha messed up, though. She told me she was sorry, and, I quote, "You can fuck any of my niggas you want. That way, we can be even." That was consent in my eyes to have sex with Tyrone, her baby's daddy, later in life.

She never put any restrictions on him. When she gave me permission to "fuck one of her niggas," she was sure none of them would ever pick me over her. Look how the tables have turned.

Being cool with Keisha is what really led me to accepting a scholarship to whatever university was furthest away from California. I vowed never to come back to this hellhole until I could sit on my high horse and look down on them like ants . . . and that is just what I have done.

I accepted an academic scholarship to Georgia Tech, in the heart of Atlanta, and graduated with a BA in business. I later received my master's in business with a minor in accounting at Tennessee State University.

Say what you must about Nashville, but if it was good enough for Oprah, it was good enough for Savannah. It made me feel like I was close to my mother living in Georgia and Tennessee, her two favorite places. I loved, and still love, both cities. Guess the apple didn't fall that far from the tree.

I was able to become someone new. No one knew me, so I didn't have to hide what I was doing. For eight years, I managed to be in relationships with men and women without anyone knowing.

I had become the top accountant at Williams and Williamson Accounting Firm in Atlanta and grossed 90K a year before my personal life started to catch up with me. I had also become a high-class ho. No one knew I was hoeing but me, and I'm my own best friend. Who would I tell?

I started sleeping with old college professors, local policemen, city councilmen, business associates, and even clients from Interstate 75 to 24 and back. I rented an apartment in Bellevue, Tennessee, right outside of Nashville, and I owned a condo in Alpharetta, Georgia, which was twenty minutes from downtown Atlanta. I never invited anyone back to my house or to live with me. Even when my grandmother passed away, instead of moving my daddy, who was the only person still living in that house, to the South, I paid the house off, renovated it, and gave it to him.

That's another rule: Never play where you lay. If you can't afford a hotel, then do it in the car. Never bring a sex partner back to your comfort zone. You have to have peace and privacy in your home. If you live by that rule, you'll never have to worry about losing a night of sleep worrying about someone popping up uninvited or driving to your house to put your tires on flat.

Everyone you meet is not going to be *the one*, so stop giving access to your kingdom to a court jester. They are in your life for entertainment purposes only. Let them perform for you onstage, not where you wear your crown.

Bringing a sexual partner back to my house was out of the question. I had never done it before and never thought I ever would. I messed up and broke my own rule when I met Dre, which led to the reason why I moved back to Cali.

Chapter 3

Southern Hospitality

Just because you start making money doesn't mean bad habits stop. They are just easier to cover up with the money that is made. I was then, and am still, addicted to the smoke, which comes from beautiful Mary Jane leaves.

In Atlanta, it was always easy to get weed. I had a coworker who had a connect that supplied me bimonthly. We met every other Friday for lunch at Houston's and exchanged cash for a two-ounce package in the parking lot. It wasn't the same for me in Nashville.

Nashville experienced a lot of droughts. That is where your supplier's supplier has run out of product, and you're waiting on them to get more or "re-up," like they call it. I met Dre during one of these droughts.

It was Friday, and my Nashville connect told me he was out and wouldn't re-up until Monday.

With a name like MJ, he should have been ashamed of himself for not keeping weed on deck 24-7.

I was fed up with him and had decided that I was going to find some weed even if that meant driving the streets of Nashville. I threw on a pair of Apple Bottom jeans, a white and gold Apple Bottom blouse, and gold pumps to try to blend in with the locals.

I jumped on Briley Parkway and got off on Dickerson Road, which was out east. One thing that I have learned while living on this earth is that the East and South sides of major cities always seem to be the hood.

I pulled up to the gas station at the intersection where Broadmoor meets Ewing Drive to get some gas. As I was walking out the door, the aroma of marijuana hit me. It was like Grannie's Sunday dinners the way it hit my nose. Allowing my nose to lead the way, I ended up at a Grand Prix parked on the side of the gas station next to a pay phone.

Not wanting to walk to my car and take the chance of him driving off, I approached him. "Where can I get some of that at?"

He looked me up and down, checking me out completely. "My boy got some across the street. What you trying to get, sexy?"

Oh my God! He had a mouth full of gold with a dollar sign on his front tooth. I almost forgot I needed his Mississippi pimp-looking ass, but I caught myself. "How much for an ounce?"

He grabbed his phone and talked to someone in what sounded like a foreign language, which must have been Tennessee trap or drug dealer Morse code because it sure wasn't English.

"Baby girl, is that your silver 300?" I nodded yes. "Go across the street and park at the nail shop next to the chicken spot and my boy is going to pull up on you."

That's the part I hated about using a new drug dealer. What if he was an undercover police officer? I made myself find comfort in the dollar sign on his tooth and the fact he kept smoking his blunt in public like it was a Newport cigarette.

I drove across the street and parked. Like clockwork, a bright yellow Monte Carlo pulled up next to me. How do you sell drugs in a car the color of a banana on a hot summer day and expect not to get caught or be noticed? Either he kept his hustling tight or was flat-out dumb.

I lowered my windows. The driver rolled his up, got out of the car, and then looked in my direction. He didn't look directly at me. It was more like he was checking out his surroundings. He must have thought I could be the police too. I was glad the feeling was mutual.

"Unlock the door, ma." I must have been fiending for this high, because I did exactly as I was told. "Start your car up and let's hit a block."

I turned to look him in the eye to tell him I didn't know the area, but the words got stuck in my throat. He was absolutely breathtaking. He had a caramel skin tone, thick, full lips, dark brown eyes, and shoulder-length dreads.

He also had a scar under his left eye that he tried to cover up with a tattoo. That rough shit turns me on. He was wearing Curve cologne, one of my all-time favorite scents, and he was decked out in Ralph Lauren Polo from head to toe. He must have just purchased the clothing, because the XXL sticker was still on it, and he had a cell phone on his lap.

"I'm not from around here. Left or right?"

Digging in his pocket, he said, "Just go around the block once, baby. I'ma weigh it out while you driving."

He tested the scale with a nickel, reset it, and poured some weed on it. I peeked to make sure I wasn't being cheated. The scale read thirty-one point three grams.

"That's all you, baby. Slide me a hundred and we good; and trust me, I got you right. You and your man are going to thank me later for this here."

It was like a reflex the way it came from my mouth. "I don't have a man," I replied, not wanting to sound desperate. I finished my statement with, "But I got weed now, so I'm good." Then I licked my lips. That's when he finally looked at me, but briefly, and only at my lips.

"Here goes my number, baby; if you ever need to get right, give me a call. I'm Dre. I deliver, but I'm charging a fee like Pizza Hut."

I pulled up next to his car and thought of seven nasty things before he even cranked up his engine that I would do to him if he ever knocked on my door with a delivery.

I drove all the way to Bellevue wondering what sex with him would be like. I could tell by his demeanor that he liked rough sex. His walk was priceless. I loved a man who was on his shit and knew it.

Dre proved himself to be honest too, because the high I got that night was as close to a California high as I was going to get in the South. The weed was so good, I felt like I needed to be freshly bathed to keep smoking. I put it out at the halfway point, went to draw a bath, and started a load of laundry.

I took an hour-long bubble bath while listening to Babyface sing me song after song on his *Greatest Hits CD*. He had just finished telling me how he would buy my clothes, cook me dinner, and pay my rent as soon as he got home from work when I got out of the tub. I ended my bath before my body shriveled up like a raisin and lotioned down with the 100 percent Shea butter I purchased from an African sister in Atlantic Station. It worked wonders on ashy elbows and blending my skin tone.

"Damn, girl, you looking good."

I had caught a glimpse of my naked body in the mirror through the candlelight and bathroom mist. I loved what I saw, not a fat roll or dent anywhere and no ink in my skin with anybody's name or design.

My body is my temple, and I wouldn't ruin it to advertise or endorse anything or anyone. I did have my clit and belly button pierced, but only to complement my flat midsection and the beautiful, neatly shaved area below my stomach. Piercings are removable; ink under the skin is not.

Clearing up the foggy mirror, I turned in a half circle to look at my butt. I have to admit that Amir, my Jamaican fling for the last six months, was right. Anal sex did have my booty looking right. My butt had never sat up that high, nor was it ever that round. That bright yellow donkey dick he gave me worked like a charm.

I wondered if it got that big from him not wearing drawers. Whatever the cause was for his enormous girth, I was thankful he shared it with me.

One night, while he was hitting me from the back, he slid his thumb in my butt. "Let me juke that booty, mi gal."

I didn't know what the hell he was talking about, and he was still stroking in and out of me, so my concentration was on handling every deep stroke he was giving me. I would have answered yes to anything he wanted at that time, and he knew it, so he continued. Amir bent me over the bed farther and got me off my knees.

He started slapping his tongue down my spine in an exotic way that made my breathing speed up. He spread my cheeks so he could continue licking downward in a straight line. He began to lick faster and made my butt even wetter with his tongue, which was long and fat, just the way I like my dicks. I could feel it twisting in and out of my butthole in a way that would eventually make me come.

I had never been a fan of getting my salad tossed. It was a mental thing for me. I just couldn't picture anyone wanting to taste what I had eaten after it was digested and on the verge of coming back out. Amir made me change my mind. I loved it. His tongue had my hole so wet I could feel it drip past my vaginal entrance, land on my stomach, and then hit the bed.

He slowly put his girth back in me with another minute or two of stroking it. He sucked on his index and middle fingers, making them wet so he could slide them in my rear entrance. In an open-and-close scissors move, he pulled his fingers in and out, and then eased his way to the closed opening of my butt and inserted the head of his hardened meat.

I screamed out in horror. No one would have heard me over the loud maracas from the reggae music he had playing, but if they could have heard my scream, they would have thought I was being raped.

"Relax, baby; breathe slowly. It will start feeling good in a minute."

How in the hell could something that caused so much pain eventually feel so damn good? Once the head was in completely, the shaft brought me so much pleasure. I felt alive in a manner I never knew existed. I buried my face deep into the mattress and took every stroke. When I released, I released from both holes and Amir released too.

I could feel the heat from his nut all over my back. He kissed my right butt cheek and passed out next to me on the bed. Anal sex is a love/ hate relationship, but trust me, it hurts so good.

Throwing on my pink lace boy shorts with matching bra, I curled up on my couch to continue smoking the other half of my blunt while I watched whatever movie I could catch the beginning of on cable. Lucky for me, *Love Jones* had just come on. I watched that movie every day while I was in college. I even drove around Atlanta playing the soundtrack with "Rush Over" and "Hopeless" on repeat. Damn, this was going to bring back memories.

I reached for the ounce of weed on my coffee table to roll up one more blunt so I wouldn't have to get back up and miss the movie when I noticed it wasn't there.

That's when I wished my legs were long enough to kick myself in the ass. I threw all the clothes I had on in the washing machine. Right about now, my weed should be in the rinse cycle awaiting the final spin.

Just like I predicted, wet weed was spinning around the machine loosely, like freshly cut grass. "Damn." I couldn't spend the rest of the weekend in the house without weed, so I grabbed the phone and called Dre.

His delivery fee was ten dollars to Bellevue since I was buying another ounce. It should have been free. It was going on 11:00 p.m., the movie was going off, and he still wasn't there. I thought it was thirty minutes or less or your delivery was free. I talked to him two hours earlier and he said, "I got two bites to catch first; then I'm headed your way." Those must have been some big bites.

By the time he called me from the security gate, I had forgotten he was coming. "Who is it?"

Then I heard that raspy voice again. "It's Dre. Buzz me in."

I buzzed the gate, and then ran to my bedroom, threw on some shorts and a baby doll T-shirt, and went to the window to watch him pull in.

If he was by himself, I would let him come up. Otherwise, I was headed downstairs. He jumped out of his car before I even told him I was letting him in. Men . . . They always assume your next move will best suit them. If I didn't need that weed, I would have told him a thing or two.

I was peeping out the hole in my door when I heard him say, "Are you going to open this door or keep peeking out your peephole at me?"

I didn't even see him standing there, to be honest. What was the point in having a non-working peephole? I'd have to speak with maintenance about that in the morning. I opened the door, but blocked the entrance with my body.

"Look, if you think I'm going to rob you, you shouldn't have invited me out here."

I scooted over slowly, tried to think of something smart to say in return, but I couldn't. It was like he had the mute button for my smart-ass mouth.

Moving me out of the way in my own apartment, he sat down on my couch, pulled out his scales again, and began his weighing routine.

"Damn, girl, you smoked that ounce already?" I still seemed to be on mute. "And this is a nice-ass spot you got here. I just might change my mind and rob you after all. I want that TV."

I explained my laundry accident to him and told him he could steal anything else in my house but my sixty-two-inch TV. I'd kill over it.

"Still, baby, you spent $200 with me in one day. I feel like I owe you something. Wanna match a blunt?" Dre must have thought I was stupid since I'd been on mute.

"Naw, I'm going to hold on to mines, but we can smoke one of yours." I joined him on the couch.

"So, you know my name. What's yours?" Still no eye contact. He hadn't looked me in my eyes since we met. That was a good thing because my anger over the lack of eye contact took me off mute.

"Don't try to pretend like this is personal, Dre, or whatever you go by. You haven't made eye contact with me since we met. You're here for the money, not to make a new friend, and my name is Savannah, or you can call me the weed head you just made $200 off of."

Now *that* seemed to get his attention. He stopped breaking down his weed and sat back, eyeing me. I finally got some eye contact. "Girl, you hell. Where are you from? That ain't a real Southern accent."

The smile that graced his lips gave me a flashback of all seven of those nasty things I thought about doing to him earlier. "I speak English properly and smoke a lot of weed. You tell me where I'm from."

Looking into my eyes again, he said, "What part of California? And what are you doing down here?"

Not wanting to go into a history lesson or give a full background check on myself, I answered, "Los Angeles and college. What about you? Are you from Nashville?"

Sparking up the blunt and taking a hit, he said, "Yep, born and raised in Jo Johnson projects 'til they tore them down. Then I moved on campus, and now I'm back out east."

Campus? Did he mean like a jail campus or college campus? I gave him the benefit of the doubt and assumed he was talking about college.

"What college did you go to?"

He had this "I really don't want to have this conversation" look on his face. "I graduated from TSU with a degree in criminology. Naw, I ain't doing shit with it because I make more money as a criminal than studying them, and let's just leave it at that." It was a touchy subject, but at least he was educated.

I inhaled the blunt he rolled and instantly realized it was different than the weed he sold me. It was Cali midgrade.

"Why didn't you sell me any of this?"

He thought it was funny and started laughing. "I don't get high on my own supply. Got to keep the best for myself. If you're really interested in getting some of this, I might be able to get you an ounce for $200. Just let me know."

The price of weed in the South is almost double the West Coast. If I trusted any of those sorry-ass guys from my old neighborhood, I would tell them to come down here, set up shop, and make a killing. But why should I look out for them when they never looked out for me?

Flipping through the channels in hopes of finding another good movie, Dre asked me to go back to that new Will Smith movie where everyone turned into zombielike creatures, and he was trying to find a cure for them.

"That movie isn't free. It costs four dollars ninety-nine cents. That's Pay-Per-View, and you don't pay the bill to view anything."

He stood up and handed me a twenty-dollar bill. "Let's watch it. I'ma go grab my Rémy outta the car since you ain't offered me nothing to drink with your rude, Californian ass. Then you can order it."

Dre had nerve, and I was feeling it, but who invited him to crash my movie/smoke night? "So, I take it you assumed I'm okay with you chilling with me because we smoked a blunt together?"

He walked out of the door like I didn't say anything to him. I watched him out of the window as he grabbed a brown bag out of his truck, rolled his car windows up, turned the alarm on, and headed back up.

There was a delay before he walked back in. Peeping out my peephole hoping to see him this time, I still wasn't able to see him. I cracked the door and looked out. He was outside on the walkway, making phone call after phone call. I could barely hear what he was saying over the TV, so I turned it down.

When I made it back to the door, I caught the end of his walkie-talkie conversation with some guy named Mike. It went like this:

Mike: "So, you ain't going to the club?"

Dre: "Naw, something came up. I'ma get with you tomorrow, though."

Mike: "This ain't like you. You sure you straight?"

Dre: "I'm good. Just make sure you count that money. If he ain't got the whole $1,500, the deal is off."

Mike: "I got you, but what you want me to tell Tasha?"

Dre: "Tell her I got a run to make, and I might not make it back to the Ville 'til the morning."

Mike: "All right."

It sounded like he had some business to handle at the club that night but decided to stay here to watch a movie with me. I wondered who Tasha was.

I went to the kitchen and got us each a glass of ice so it wouldn't look like I was eavesdropping. Then I grabbed my bottle of white wine and met up with him at the couch.

"To answer your question, yes, I think I'm chilling with you tonight. I don't feel like the club scene, and I ain't sat back and watched a movie in a minute. If you got somebody coming by, let me know and I'll bounce."

I shook my head and handed him his glass. What was he doing to me? I'd lost my bark and bite since he had been there. I needed to say something. "I didn't really want to watch a movie alone tonight, so it's cool you decided to stay." *What in the hell was that, Savannah? It sounded too sensitive. Try again, girl, damn!* "Plus, I've been wanting to see this movie and been refusing to pay for it, so thanks for the twenty bucks, and it wouldn't hurt if you rolled up another blunt. I would offer to match you, but my supplier sold me some bullshit." Now, *that's* better, girl. I couldn't believe I was coaching myself on how to handle the man.

I broke down a cigar and handed it to him. While he rolled up, I ordered the movie and went to grab a few pillows from my bed for my back.

I noticed he was watching me, not in an untrusting way, but as if he was staring at my butt. When I came back, he was smoking and watching the movie.

We sat in silence for about thirty minutes, and then the alert on his phone went off. He checked the number, then put it back down. Five minutes or so later, his phone was ringing off the hook. There must have been ten calls back-to-back that he just ignored. Finally, a woman's voice chirped through on his walkie-talkie.

"Dre, where are you? Why are you not answering my calls?"

He looked at me as if he thought I would say something, and then grabbed his phone. "I told you I had business to handle tonight. What's up?"

The woman wasted no time on her response. "My mama got the baby so I thought I'd come to the club and surprise you, but Mike said you went somewhere else. Where you at?"

He looked at me again. "I had to run to Kentucky. I'll see you in the morning."

An unrelieved and disappointed voice said, "Uh-huh, okay," and hung up.

Before he tried to explain, I looked at him and said, "That ain't none of my business." He seemed to relax and got back into the movie again.

Who was I fooling? I wanted to know the details of his relationship with the woman on the other end of the phone.

Was that the Tasha his boy Mike spoke of earlier? It didn't matter to me anyway, but it would be nice if he offered the information.

Not only was I high, but now I was drunk. I drank the entire 750 ml bottle myself, and now I had to pee.

I tried to get up and go to the bathroom without him noticing I was intoxicated, but falling back down after standing up didn't help me hide it at all.

"I got you, Savannah." Grabbing me by my waist, he asked, "Where you trying to go?"

I pointed to the bathroom. He led me there, and then closed the door behind me. I used the bathroom, flushed the toilet, and had started washing my hands when the door flew open.

"You ready to get back on the couch?" He was there to help me. "Look, if you don't mind, I'ma crash on your floor until you sober up some. It was funny as hell when you just fell, but I don't want you to hurt yourself."

Was he sober? The Rémy bottle was empty too, and we had smoked three blunts within two hours. I almost applauded him for being concerned, until he admitted my fall brought him laughter. However, I needed the help, and I wasn't ready for him to leave, anyway. Drunk and all, I was getting some dick from him tonight.

"I have a two-bedroom. You can use the guest bedroom, if you like."

He agreed to sleep in the guest bedroom but wanted to watch ESPN before calling it a night.

"Damn, the Cavs got put out of the playoffs again. LeBron can't do it by himself." Was he a LeBron James fan? Okay, I'd heard enough.

"No, he's not Kobe."

That seemed to spark up conversation all over again. We went back and forth over the players' stats, teammates, and coaches. We must have spent an additional hour talking about the league in general and all the changes that had been made over the last fifteen years.

He argued me down that Iverson's crossover was not a carry. I slipped up and told him I played ball and got the call placed on me every time I did it.

"You played? Who did you play for and what position?"

I didn't answer. Instead, I sparked up a conversation about Penny Hardaway to throw him off course. The conversation seemed to sober us up, and we decided to smoke one more blunt, which was not a good idea.

The talk of basketball alone was enough to get me wet, but adding weed to the equation made it worse. Drunken, I told him how all the basketball talk had turned me on and how I'd wanted to do nasty things to him since I had met him. I became dominant and informed him that he was giving up the dick whether or not he liked it.

I've always had a potty mouth but tried to contain it around people I didn't know. But there was something about Dre that made me feel relaxed and comfortable enough to be myself.

I don't remember all the details of how I let it all out, but I do remember inviting him to sleep in my bed with me if he wanted a sample of those "nasty things." I was the aggressor in the beginning, but he soon took the torch from me and put out my flame.

"There's something about you too that got a nigga wanting to see what you're about. But I ain't no petty-ass nigga, so I'ma wait 'til you're sober to get that sample. I do wanna lie with you tonight, though. I don't get no sleep where I stay 'cause I ain't comfortable, and I've been comfortable 'round you all night. I'm not shooting you down, beautiful, just taking a rain check."

Did he just turn me down out of respect for me? I was lost for words. I didn't know if I was happy or pissed off about it.

I took my shirt and shorts off and got into the bed. He joined me in boxers and a wife beater. He placed my head on his chest and was out like a light.

Chapter 4

So Typical

In the morning, I woke up to an empty bed, but could hear the woman's voice from last night in my living room.

"So, how long you gon' be in Texas? Why can't you send Mike on the run? I'm so tired of you always traveling. I wish you was back in jail. At least you would stay in one damn place, Dre."

In the sexiest morning voice I've ever heard in my life, he said, "Damn, you want a nigga to go to jail, huh? Look, I'll see you Monday. Kiss my son and tell him Daddy loves him. I'm done talking to yo' stupid ass."

I heard his phone power off and him start walking back to my bedroom. He was still in his boxers and beater when he walked back into the room.

"Good morning," I said to let him know I was up.

"Good morning, Miss Savannah, did you sleep well?" he asked, while pointing to the wet spot on his beater that I must have made drooling on it.

"I'm sorry. I guess I did." I was blushing so hard my cheeks started hurting.

"Throw on some sweats and a T-shirt and let's go have breakfast, beautiful."

He put on his clothes from the night before, went downstairs to his car, and came back up with a black duffle bag. He removed a facecloth and toothbrush and began brushing his teeth. I joined him in the restroom and brushed mine.

Looking at him, I said, "I'm sorry about last night. I didn't mean to say all that stuff to you."

Rinsing his mouth out, he said, "I was hoping you did mean it," with a smile.

I dressed quickly, and we headed out the door. I suggested we go in my car, since I was more familiar with the area. He agreed, then grabbed my car keys and said he was driving. We pulled into Waffle House.

"Dre, I don't eat here. It doesn't look safe, and it is nowhere near having even two stars, let alone five."

He shook his head. "You gon' eat here today." After five minutes of debating, he won, and we walked in and sat on stools.

He ordered for both of us. Not even five minutes later, our food came. He prayed over it and fed me my first spoon of smothered and covered hash browns. I was shocked at how good they were.

"So, since we slept together, I think it's time you tell me more about yourself, and you can start off with telling me who that woman was that called last night."

He ate two more bites of his raisin toast, and then began talking. He told me it was his son's mother. They had been dating for two years, and his son was now one year old. The love had gone, but he still cared and took care of her as if it never left. He tried to end it many times, but whenever he did, she cut him out of his son's life, so he played the role to see his son.

The heartbreaker for me was that they lived together. He had in-house pussy. He didn't want his son to grow up without him, and applying for full custody wouldn't be a smart thing to do in his line of work. He went further to tell me that they met while he was in jail. She had written and visited him for two years before they hooked up. She refused to start a relationship with him behind bars.

Sounded like a smart woman. There is no way I would be faithful to a man that was behind bars.

I'm not holding it down while a man is locked up. I would be dating somebody else before his first court date.

After paying the bill, he asked where the nearest grocery store was. I directed him to Kroger, and when we walked in, he asked if I liked seafood. I said, "I love it." He spent seventy dollars on lobster tails and shrimp, and then grabbed a few other items.

"So, I take it you will be here for dinner?"

He took my face in his hand and said, "I'm hoping to be here for two dinners and another breakfast."

My blood started running hot. I had never spent that much time with a man I didn't know before, and all common sense flew out the door. I was enjoying his company and glad he was enjoying mine. I had only received that type of attention from a man *after* we had sex. If he was like this now, I know he would be even better after I gave him some of the goods.

We were talking politics when his phone rang. He listened briefly, and then yelled, "What the hell you mean? I'm on my way."

On the ride back to my apartment, he said he had to go handle some business and would be back. I felt like breaking his phone. I pretended to understand, but I really didn't. I parked my car and carried the bags up as he drove 50 mph out of my complex.

I tried to guess what the other person had said to him on the other end of the phone, but had no clue what it could have been. When you live the lifestyle he lived, anything was possible.

I wondered if his baby mama made up something to get his attention. Women are good for faking tragedies to gain the attention of men. I've seen some good acting too. The classic flat-tire routine or, my all-time favorite, "the baby is sick" trick. Dealing with married men and men with baby mamas has allowed me to see it all. Woman will do anything to get a man's attention, even if it meant using the kids as bait.

I showered, and then put out an all-black Baby Phat dress that my secretary, Stephanie, had given me for my birthday. I had never worn the dress because when I cut off the sex she requested, we kept everything business from then on out. I couldn't see myself wearing it and having her think I was still interested in her. Don't get lost in my words . . . The sex was good, but that's all it was to me—nothing but sex.

I laid silver accessories out next to it and a pair of sterling silver earrings I had bought from Macy's. If he was to come back, my hair and makeup would be at its best. Just in case he wanted that sample tonight, I would wax all the important areas and make sure they were baby-powder fresh.

I needed somebody to talk to. I felt like I was going to explode if I didn't tell somebody about Dre. I don't do the girl talk thing, but I needed to tell someone what had happened in the last twenty-four hours, so I called my best friend, Sandy, whom I graduated from Georgia Tech with. Due to her living in France now, we didn't talk like we used to, but she was the only person who knew the real me.

I gave her the rundown and waited on her opinion. "Savannah, you ain't never let no man get to you like this. You sure you should let him come back? What if there is more to that baby-mama thing then he let on? I thought that Jamaican guy was packing enough for you and me both." Never ask for someone's opinion when you know you really don't want to hear it. "And how is he going to be more comfortable at your house than his own? You sure he ain't got people looking for him, girl?"

That was so typical of Sandy to turn every thuggish guy she knew into somebody wanted on *Cops* or *The First 48*. I loved her because she always spoke her mind, regardless of whether your feelings were going to get hurt.

"I'm not worried about his baby mama. We're not talking about marriage. I'm just curious if he can really cook and if his sex is as smooth as he is. As far as Amir goes, I told him I wasn't looking for anything but sex every now and then. We're on the same page." I decided not to tell her that I planned on cooking the food and having the house covered in candles by the time he made it back.

"Okay, Savannah, I know you know what you're doing. Get enough for me. I've been working so much I haven't even had time to masturbate."

Sandy worked for a historian, rejuvenating priceless artifacts without taking away from their worth. Her job took a lot of concentration and attention to detail. I missed her dearly, but I knew our schedules didn't allow for frequent visits, so I promised to visit on my next vacation and said good-bye.

At about a quarter to five, I received a text message from Dre asking if it was okay to come back at 8:00 p.m. I texted back: Yes, and come hungry.

I started cooking dinner, and then got dressed. The dress fit my body like a glove. I must thank Stephanie for it again. I changed my mind about wearing heavy makeup and only applied eye shadow and a thin layer of lip gloss. My hair was easy to do since it was so short. Next, I slipped on my heels. Right as I dropped the lobsters in the boiling water, I got a call from the security gate.

Dre was almost an hour early, which worked out fine since the only things that needed to be cooked were the lobster tails. He had bought the frozen, precooked ones, so they only needed ten minutes of boiling.

I buzzed him in, and then peeked out of the window. He had changed clothes. He was now wearing a long-sleeved Christian Audigier shirt with matching jeans. It was hard to see what kind of shoes he was wearing, but they matched in color. He had his dreads pulled back and his cell phone stuck to his ear.

As I walked to the door to unlock it, I could hear his cell phone powering off. Thank you, Jesus. No more unwanted interruptions. I opened up the door. "Welcome back."

Looking like an embarrassed child by the way he put his head down, he said, "Glad to be welcomed back."

I led him into the dimly lit dining area and sat him down. His eyes followed me all around the kitchen. "It smells good in here, Savannah. Who you pay to cook while I was gone?"

Giving him the middle finger, I placed jumbo shrimp, asparagus, and three-cheese mashed potatoes on his plate. I did the same for myself as the lobster tails continued to cook.

I handed him a bottle of red wine to open, and he poured us a glass, and then sparked up a blunt. He hit it three times and passed it and told me to put it out when I was done. I did.

As I walked to my side of the table to sit down, he beat me there and pulled out my chair. After I was seated, we prayed over the food.

"Savannah, I got to be real with you. I had dreams of having a meal like this with a beautiful and educated woman like yourself when I was in college, and the shit never happened. So you got to excuse me if it seems like I'm overdoing it."

I sipped my wine and said, "Just be you. That's who I want to get to know."

Over dinner, he told me what the call was about. It seemed his boy, Mike, had accepted $1,200 for some product that he was expecting $1,500 for. He not only got the missing $300 back, but also convinced the guy to spend an additional $1,000 with him.

Drug-selling stories don't impress me. I didn't stop him because he was giving me all the details of his day, which prevented me from asking why he didn't hurry back. Dre had so much potential.

If he would just get a real job and start over, we might be able to date.

Once dinner was done, he insisted on washing the dishes while I found a NBA playoff game to watch. He joined me on the couch and pulled me closer to him. I heard him breathe in deeply, and then watched his pants rise.

I was wearing "Love Spell," and it looked like he was under my magic. I placed my hand on his zipper, rubbing softly to acknowledge his hard-on. He kissed my neck. I looked up at him, and he grabbed my face and started kissing me long and hard.

His mouth tasted so good, and his lips were soft and sweet, like the wine we had been drinking. His pants rose higher, so I freed the beast from his cage and let him run free.

What a beautiful piece of artwork he had hiding beneath his pants. It must have been nine inches, and it didn't curve at all. His balls were evenly proportioned on each side. It was a masterpiece. I fell to my knees and swallowed the whole thing. It fit perfectly down my throat.

Going up and down on his shaft, adding more in my mouth with every bob of my head, I started sucking on the head of it, and then going right back down until my chin rested in his hairs, which were neatly trimmed. Covering his girth in my saliva, I stroked it with my hands as I placed both of his balls in my mouth. He let out a deep moan.

"Damn, you're beautiful." He said this when our eyes met and my mouth was filled to capacity with his balls.

I started sucking his girth again, this time much faster and a lot wetter than before. I moaned and played with my clit as I sucked it. He pulled it out of my mouth, and then laid me on the floor.

Sliding his hands up my legs, he removed my panties and began licking my pearl tongue and sucking on it with his lips at the same time. The vibration his mouth was giving off sent chills throughout my entire body. "You even taste sweet, baby," he moaned. He went back down and started all over again with the licking and sucking. He then nibbled on my inner lips from side to side.

I couldn't take it anymore. "I want it, Dre. What are you waiting for?"

He dug in his back pocket and came out with a condom. Lifting my dress over my head, he kissed both of my hard nipples while putting the condom on. He squeezed both of my breasts together and placed both nipples into his mouth, sucking hard. Using his legs to spread my legs, he put the tip of his rock-solid dick in me. Dre threw out the thirty-second rule within the first five strokes, causing me to come and shake from his first deep stroke.

He tucked my thighs into the folds of his arms and went deeper. I don't know what he hit, but it made tears roll out of my eyes. Wiping my eyes with his index fingers, he buried his face into my breasts. This went on for about twenty minutes; then he flipped me on top of him.

I became the cowgirl I was used to being. I rode him from the bottom of his shaft and back up, then circled around his head and dropped back down. My hands rested on his almond-colored chest. I grinded hard and used my hips to make him squint his eyes. "Hell, naw, this shit ain't going to work."

He flipped me on my stomach and hit me doggie style while talking shit the whole time. "So you thought you was going to ride me and make me nut, huh? You can forget that. I'm going to be inside you 'til the sun comes up."

I bit the throw rug on the floor in hopes of covering up the scream I felt coming, but it didn't work. "Damn, Dre, shit!" The words felt perfect flowing out of my mouth. He put my arms together by my elbows and banged my back out.

"You're going to be mine, ain't that right?" I didn't answer, so he went deeper. "I said ain't that right, Savannah?" His sex was off the chain.

I screamed out, "Yes!" I wasn't sure if I meant it or not, but we could work something out. He pulled his dick out of me and began slapping my ass with it.

"Damn, this pussy good. Get back on your back. Let me see how much you can take."

I should have stayed on my knees. When I got back in the missionary position, there was nothing missionary about it.

There was something about the word *pussy* and the way Dre said it that was sexier to me than anything else you can call it. There was a dirtier feel about it, no more daddy's little girl. He said it like there was a desire and a craving for my pussy and me. For that moment in time, in the arms of a real man, I felt like I was a woman. Pure feline with the heart of a lion. Like a wildcat—free and able to be me. There was a completeness to that very same moment our cocoa-butter skin tones met that let me know the Queen had met her King.

The way the word slid out of his mouth made me want to be as free as I wanted to be sexually with him, but there was one problem. Dre was working with way too much. He dug his girth so deep inside of me that his balls rested in between my butt checks, and I couldn't move.

"Dre, you're too deep!" I screamed out.

He just smiled like he was possessed and said, "No, I ain't, because you're still awake. Got to go into overtime; forgot you're an athlete."

I don't remember how it ended because I was awakened by the same thing that caused me to go to sleep—him fucking the shit out of me.

It had to be about eight in the morning before he actually called it quits, and I only know that because his phone rang and I opened my eyes to glance at the clock. He must have turned his phone back on while I was asleep. All I know is that when I woke up around noon, I was naked, uncovered, and alone.

After I soaked in the tub to try to help heal the soreness from the beating I received, I called Dre's cell, but there was no answer. I waited an hour and tried again; still no answer. I didn't want to look attached, so I decided not to call him again until I had washed all my clothes and packed for my trip back home to Atlanta.

I kept watching the clock. It seemed like the time was going by slowly. It had only been an hour since my last attempt to reach Dre, but it felt like days.

Okay, Savannah, get your shit together, girl. He's just another nigga. But, *was* he just another nigga? I hadn't experienced one like him before. Yes, he had some similarities to other men I dated, but that just qualified him as my type, right? I did want a man like Dre, someone who could tame my hot ass and keep me in line, but what about his baby's mama? I had so many thoughts and unanswered questions.

I heard music playing in my head: "Say Yes" by Floetry. Oh, shit, that was my phone ringing. Technically, it was my text message tone—Dre.

I hit my pinkie toe on the laundry room door frame trying to get to it. The pain shot up my leg to my knee and brought me down hard to the floor. I didn't have time to nurse the pain. I had to get to that phone. I scooted across the floor until I reached the couch and grabbed my phone.

To my disappointment, it was Sandy, texting me to get the details of my night with Dre. I threw the phone back down. I wasn't in the mood for girl talk at all.

I know I promised to wait before I called again, but a text message was not considered a call, now, was it? I texted: I'm heading home tonight and would like to see you before I leave if possible.

Do you know I waited *four hours* and did not get a return text? Who in the hell did he think I was? I went from anger to concern and back. It was time to get on the road if I was going to make it home at a decent hour, but I didn't want to miss his return if there was going to be one, so I decided to take off on Monday.

I sat on the couch until I fell asleep, waiting on Dre. I woke up from hearing the kids in my complex grouping up to walk to their school buses. I waited until seven o'clock before I dialed his number. Once again, I was forwarded to voice mail. I was planning to leave a fuck-you message, but decided to play it cool.

"Hey, Dre, just wanted to thank you again for all the great Southern hospitality. See you around."

I grabbed my shit, erased his number out of my phone, and headed to my car to leave Tennessee behind. Fuck Dre.

Chapter 5

The Intrusion

When I got back to Alpharetta, I had so many voice messages on my house phone it was unbelievable. Sandy was nosier than I thought. I had five messages from her telling me that she needed all the dirty details and if I didn't call her back, she was on her way.

I had a "Just checking on you" message from my daddy. He must have called my office looking for me, and I was right because my last message was from Stephanie telling me my father called saying he was worried sick about me because he hadn't heard from me in two weeks.

I called him to calm his nerves. Since Memphis had been shot in the leg, he had called me once a week and that happened over three years earlier. Memphis was selling dope and got shot, which is a different life than I lived, but I made sure to give him safety updates so he could have peace of mind.

I was glad I took the day off. It gave me time to take a few items to the cleaners and prepare for a hell of a workweek. I had final contract meetings with two of my six-figure clients on Friday, and I wanted to work on my proposal, correcting any weaknesses I had overlooked.

While walking out of Starbucks from getting my daily Mocha Frappuccino, I got a call from Dre.

"Hey, baby, how you are?"

The sound of his voice made all the anger I had in me come back, but I still needed to play smooth. "Hey."

There was a pause after my response, and then he said, "I got your calls, messages, and shit, but you know Sundays are family days, so everything else gets put on hold. But I wanted to see you too. Where you at?"

I took a deep breath and tried hard not to snap. "I'm in Atlanta getting myself ready for work. Look, Dre, what do you want from me? I need to know, because it sounds like you, your son, and your baby mama got everything squared away."

He cleared his throat. "My baby mama and son ain't got shit to do with me and you, and I know you upset at how I just shook you without a good-bye, but my life with them comes first. Now it's your time, baby. Are you going to invite me to Atlanta tonight or what?"

Instead of replying, I just hung up. Dre was trouble. He made me feel so weak and dumb minded, and that was not a comfortable feeling.

He didn't try to call back, and I'm glad he didn't. I stopped at Justin's, grabbed a to-go order, and ate in front of the TV alone. My peaceful meal was interrupted by a call from Mike, Dre's boy.

"Is this Savannah?"

Still staring at my phone, I said, "This is her." I couldn't believe he had his boy do his dirty work. I hoped he wasn't calling to confront me about hanging up the phone, because we could have a repeat of that incident right now.

"Ay, this is Mike, Dre's friend. We met at the gas station. Anyways, my boy asked me to call you and tell you to meet him at your place in four hours. I can't go into details, but he said he needs you. Tell me you coming."

I don't know if it was curiosity or the urgency in his voice that made me get up. "Tell him I'm on my way," I said, grabbing my purse and shoes. I shot down to my Charger. It had a full tank, and it was faster than the 300. I made it all the way to Chattanooga before I thought about work.

"Stephanie, are you awake?" I hated to call her, but she was the only person who could rearrange my schedule and help me get prepared for Friday. I told her that I had to get some things together in Nashville and wouldn't be back until Thursday evening.

I asked her to get my slides together on the PowerPoint we had been working on, to cancel any lunch dates I had on Tuesday, Wednesday, and Thursday, and to respond to all inquiries that were over $50,000. I reminded her to send all my clients their annual thank-you cards and goody baskets filled with everything they liked personally. I could hear her writing away as I gave her instruction after instruction. That was one of the things that led me to sleeping with her. She knew her job and was good at it, which was a turn-on for me.

Stephanie came to me through a temp agency. After her first week of work, I knew I wanted to hire her as my permanent secretary. She was efficient, fast, and knew how to stay a step ahead of my needs. I would have never made a sexual pass at her. I had an office full of sexual harassment videos given to me by HR, and I memorized each one of them. Luckily, for me, she came by my house one Saturday afternoon to drop off some dry cleaning she had picked up for me.

She was wearing an Ann Klein Summer Collection yellow dress with sandals. Her hair was pulled back to the side in a ponytail that allowed her hair to fall over her right shoulder. I had never seen her without a business suit on.

As she walked up the pathway to my condo, I could see her hips and breasts protruding from her dress. Her nipples were hard like it was below zero outside. She was bad, with skin the same tone as honey, and I bet she dripped slowly like it.

She followed me into my house and laid my clothing across the couch. Bending slightly, I could see how round her ass really was. She caught me staring, so I turned my head to play it off.

"You can look. I've been hoping you would."

Trying to play confused, I said, "What are you talking about?"

She walked up to me, kissed my lips, and said, "I've been waiting a year for you to look at me that way."

I couldn't muster up anything to say back except, "Is that right?"

Nodding her head, she took a step closer. "I saw your schedule was empty today and thought I'd pencil myself in. I hope you don't mind."

Hell, she managed my schedule. She could have penciled herself in a long time ago. What was so different about now? Before I even asked, I thought about it. Last week, I stopped sleeping with Angel from the gym. I had Stephanie order the flowers, and they included a breakup card.

"Do you know I could fire you right now for this?"

She didn't seem concerned. In fact, she took a step closer, and that was all she wrote. I took her down right by the living-room door. She was saying all kinds of shit to me, but I wasn't listening, I just wanted the warmth in between her legs.

She soon became my fill-in sex or, at least, that's how I saw her. Whenever I wanted some and didn't have a candidate, I would invite her over.

Everything was going good until I had her invite Gina, the Latino freak I met at the store, to lunch for me. She set the first date up for me with all smiles. By the third meeting, I was being questioned about my plans with Gina. I know a red flag when I see one. So I called our sex sessions off.

I don't do titles with women or men, nor do I have plans on being faithful to either sex. The mentality I have when it comes to women prevents me from trying to do serious relationships with men. I'm sure they look at me the same way that I look at women, which is that pussy is a rare fruit and you will never run across the same taste or feel twice. So I collect each like a merit badge like I'm in the Girl Scouts. Life is much easier when you're free, and I'd be damned before I locked myself down with one person, especially a woman.

Maybe I was lonely or just had a lot of errands that week, because I stayed on the phone with Stephanie until I reached my apartment complex. When I drove in, Dre was already parked in front of my unit.

"Thanks, Steph, I got to go." I pulled up next to him and went upstairs. He followed closely behind me. As soon as we walked in the door, he pulled me into his arms and kissed me.

"Thank you, baby, I knew you wouldn't let me down."

I enjoyed the kiss, but I had just finished driving three and a half hours. He had some explaining to do. I pushed him off me. "So, I'm here. What was so urgent?"

Walking me over to the couch, he told me the person he had Mike meet at the club, the one who tried to cheat him out of $300, got busted after getting that additional $1,000 worth of product from him. Word around town was that dude was going to give up Dre and his supplier for an easier sentence since he was a parolee.

"Wow. Dre, I hate to hear that!"

"Yeah, me too. They're going to put my life on pause like I can get the time back and make me sit down for a while. This shit is crazy."

He kept going with his situation, but I now had my own problems. Where would I meet another nigga like Dre? Not only was I losing a potential fling, but also some of the best head I had ever gotten in Tennessee. That was so messed up. I didn't care about his problems. All I could think about was how I was supposed to move on after meeting a man like him.

I decided to let him hide out until I left Thursday night so I could get three days of his body before it belonged to the state of Tennessee. I felt the old me coming back. Fuck Dre. He was no better than the niggas I grew up around.

When I went off to college, Memphis started selling drugs and was arrested. If I didn't visit, write, or accept my own brother's phone calls, I wasn't about to do it for anybody else.

This is why I don't get attached to people. They always seem to let you down. As long as I have myself, to hell with everybody else. I don't even want kids. They are too needy and stressful. I'll spend sixteen years getting attached to them and catering to their needs hand and foot, only to watch them pick their friends over me.

Fuck that. I wouldn't dare kill my figure for stretch marks and changing shitty diapers. I'll leave the entire baby-having thing to my fat and ugly friends. I can be a godmother or something.

I felt something with Dre that I never felt with anyone before and in a few days, it would be just another memory. I was going to enjoy the last three days of Dre, and when I left Tennessee, it would be like he never existed.

Pretending I was listening the entire time, I cut him off. "I'll take the next few days off of work, baby, and you can stay here with me. That will give you some time to come up with your next move."

The next three days went by too quickly. I guess that's because all we did was sleep, eat, and make love. I was really starting to like Dre. He was more intelligent than I had gathered. Once he was forced to get away from his drug-dealer role, he became more my type, which made me glad that in a few hours he would be out of my life as if I never met him—or so I thought.

Never in a million years would I have thought one man, who I'd known for less than a week, would change the entire flow of my life.

To prevent the chance of him trying to contact me, I called my cell phone provider and had my number changed. I called all the important contacts in my phone and gave them my new number. They were used to my number being changed because I seemed to run across a lot of people who didn't understand what "leave me the hell alone" means.

I had been out of my one-year lease with my apartment complex in Bellevue for a while and was on a month-to-month basis with them. I called and informed them that I wouldn't be renting from them after that month. That gave me three weeks to get my things out of that apartment, which was more than enough time to hire professional movers.

There was no way in hell I was going to continue living in that apartment complex after meeting Dre. I didn't trust him, and the lack of eye contact he gave me let me know he didn't trust me, either, which was fine with me.

I normally went into details about my job or what it is that I do for a living, but with Dre, I didn't share a thing. It wouldn't take much to disappear from him, just get a new telephone number and address.

The night after I left him, I couldn't sleep. I kept having horrible dreams about pregnancy, unemployment, getting married to Dre while he was in jail, and fighting during jailhouse visits with his baby mama. I didn't like the fact that I had cut him off, yet he lingered in my dreams. How do I convince myself that I am done with him? It was the best sex I ever had in my life, and I got three days' worth of it. Of course, he was still going to be on my mind.

It was an hour before my alarm clock would go off, and I refused to sit around with thoughts of Dre for another hour. I got up, got myself together for work, and by the time my alarm did go off, I was twenty minutes away from walking out of the door.

I headed to Starbucks for a Frappuccino and cream cheese Danish, and then headed to work. Once I made it to work, I decided to order Stephanie flowers to thank her for picking up my slack for the last four days. She had completed every task I requested to be done and went beyond by also setting up the conference room for my meeting. She had the PowerPoint set up on the computer, all the slides were numbered and organized, and she even supplied me with a cheat sheet, which highlighted all the crucial points I needed to make. She had made my presentation easy for me. All I had to do was present the information and pray that it was enough to close the deal.

"Knock knock, did someone in this here office send me flowers?" she was standing in my door with her face buried in her dozen of dark pink roses.

"Yes, I did. I know I don't tell you often enough, but I really appreciate all you do for me on and off the clock." I gave her a wink, and she dove deeper into their contagious scent to try to hide the rosy glow warming her cheeks.

"They are beautiful. The last time I was given flowers it was from you to deliver to one of your flings with a 'I'm cutting you off' heartbreak letter. I checked my flowers for an identical card but didn't find one."

She turned on her heels like a solider with a full-toothed smile on her face to exit but never took a step. She looked back at me.

"Oh, I almost forgot to tell you, your apartment complex in Tennessee has been blowing me up looking for you. I told them I'd tell you when you made it to work. Girl, I checked the office messages and they had already left four by eight o'clock our time. Isn't Nashville on central time? They didn't give any details or say what it was that they wanted, but it must be important if they're blowing up every number they have for you before seven o'clock. Please hurry and call them folks back so they can leave me alone. Do you need the number?"

"No, I have it and thanks again for everything, Steph."

"No problem at all and you're welcome."

I wondered what they could have wanted, but I needed to eat and get familiar with my presentation. It wasn't like them to call me on the job. Even when they had to do maintenance work, they called my cell phone. Maybe they had attempted to call my disconnected number.

I had gone five hours without thinking about Dre. The only reason he crossed my mind now was because the apartment employees kept calling me, and my move was an attempt to erase him. I decided to return their call as soon as the meeting was over.

The meeting started promptly at 2:00 p.m. If it went smoothly, it should be over by 3:30 p.m. at the latest. Everything was going as planned. The prospective clients seemed impressed with the layout of their financial data. It was almost 3:30 p.m., and I had every question answered.

"Our firm in California will handle your account. Their focus will be on your business needs solely . . ."

My words were taken over as curiosity of why the receptionist, Darlene, from the first floor, walked in with two male detectives from the Atlanta Police Department. One was short and stocky. The other was an older gentleman. They were both black. Darlene nodded her head in my direction, and when the officers walked past her, she looked at me and shrugged her shoulders as if to say she had no clue of what they wanted with me.

"Are you Savannah James?" asked the older of the two detectives. As he moved closer, I saw that he looked like Don Cornelius from *Soul Train*. It was hard not to smirk as I thought of him stopping in his tracks and saying, "Love, peace, and soul." While I was daydreaming, the detectives were still waiting on a response.

"Yes, I am, and I'm in the middle of a meeting. How may I help you two gentlemen?" I don't know if the stockier detective was mute, but he never said a word.

"Mrs. James, we need to speak with you about an incident that occurred at your rental property in Tennessee involving an Andre Burns."

I jumped to my feet quickly. There was no way I was going to let Dre, Andre, or whatever the hell he went by, fuck me out of the deal with those clients. It had to have involved him. I was sure of it before they said the criminal's government name.

"It's Ms. James, and, of course."

I excused myself from the meeting and left them in Stephanie's hands. She was more than capable of handling the meeting. My concern was the future client thinking I had some criminal investigation pending.

Everyone in the office was standing on the other side of the door when I walked out with the two detectives, including Mr. Williams. He was known to be nosy, but it never bothered me because it wasn't my business he had his nose in—until then. He stopped the detectives and introduced himself as my direct superior. Without a bit of shame in his voice, he asked what was going on.

Detective Soul Train reached to shake his hand in return, and then said, "There was a break-in at her home in Tennessee, and we need to get a statement from her. She is the victim, like I'm sure you had already assumed."

Looking hot under the collar, he responded. "Of course I assumed such. Let me know if we can be of any help to you, Ms. James."

I was so glad that was over. Now the entire building—all twenty floors—would look at me like a victim instead of the criminal I was. I hadn't even been told what they wanted with me, but I knew I was guilty of whatever I was accused of. I led the way to my office and offered them both a seat.

"Ms. James, we received a call from the Nashville Metropolitan Police Department requesting we search your condo looking for an Andre Burns or drug paraphernalia. Both Atlanta PD and Tennessee investigators have searched your homes from top to bottom as we were warranted to do and have uncovered nothing but a fourth of a cigar stuffed with marijuana. You can answer our questions now or at the police station in the presence of your lawyer."

Shaking my head no, I spilled my guts before he had gotten the first question out of his mouth. I started at the gas station and ended with changing my telephone number and address. The mute detective recorded my statement and the other took notes. "So, where is he now?"

Did that motherfucker listen to *anything* I had just said? "I don't know. He went his way, and I went mine."

He handed me his card.

"We'll be in touch, but I recommend you get in contact with the Nashville Police Department before they make an attempt to get in contact with you. These things can get bad without full cooperation."

"I will immediately. Thank you."

***

I was still in shock when Stephanie came in. "What did they want with you? Are you okay? Who broke into your house?"

I saw Mr. Williams wasted no time telling everyone what happened. I couldn't think of anything to say back. I knew both of my homes had been destroyed. I had watched *Cops* enough to know what I would be facing when I made it home.

I wanted to cry, but that's a sign of weakness, and I devoted my adult life to advertising strength. Stale faced, I asked, "Can I stay with you for the weekend? I need to get away right now."

Without asking another question, she said, "Yes." I told her we would be leaving then, and to go grab her purse.

Since we would be together until Monday, I left my car, which had also been searched, in the parking garage at work and rode with her. On the ride to her house, I told her what happened as if she was the police.

"Hell, naw, Savannah. We going to your condo, and I'll have a cleaning crew meet us there." Her nickname should have been Google because when we got there, her sister, Tracey, and the cleaning crew were already there working. I had a new front door, which meant the other must have been kicked in.

"When we got here, they were putting it up. The guy said your key still works. They put the old locks on this door." When Tracey finished, she pointed to the new door frame I had. My house was a thousand times worse than I imagined.

The police had knocked over everything, even my refrigerator. They had cut every box of cake mix and bag of flour I had. My pictures were off the wall, clothes from my bedroom in the living room, and these motherfuckers had even searched my fish tank, because my Oscars were swimming around in a punch bowl. I had seen enough.

Stephanie demanded that my house be finished tonight and she told Tracey to stay there for the weekend just in case they came back. She paid everyone and ordered them pizza. "You ready to go?"

I felt like a zombie, but I followed her out of the house. Stephanie was calling the shots, and I was going to follow her lead.

"Tomorrow, after breakfast, we're heading to Tennessee so you can speak with the police; then we're calling a moving company to get your shit and follow us back here. You can put your things in my storage until you're ready to get them. I'm headed to the Liquor Bank, and I'm about to ease your mind."

She dug into her purse and held up what looked like two ounces of weed. "You thought I was going to leave him sitting at Houston's waiting on you? I keep telling you I got your back."

Damn, she had met up with Marcus to pick up my weed. I had forgotten all about him with everything going on that day. I was able to get out a "Thank you," but she talked right over it.

"I'll stop and get some cigars while we out. You're in good hands. Relax." After her many stops for food, liquor, cigars, and movies, we finally made it to her house. She had a nice two-bedroom house outside of Stone Mountain. The area wasn't all that great, but whenever I missed home, it was my comforter.

I hated to say it, but after the shit I went through that day, home was looking a lot better. Even though South Central was a rough place to live, niggas went down by themselves. They weren't trying to take nobody with them. The no-snitch rule was one rule everybody went by, and there were consequences if you didn't.

"Come eat something before you get on this liquor."

I joined her in the kitchen, sat on her counter, and murdered my food. Stephanie knew where all the good, home-style food spots were, no matter what city and state we were in. She had ordered catfish and spaghetti from a little spot near her house, and man, it was good. As I looked up, I was rubbing my sliced bread across my plate, trying to get the last taste of spaghetti off it.

I rolled up a blunt while she made the drinks, and then we smoked in the kitchen. Weed was really a cure-all for me because I started feeling like myself instantly. I got up and started rubbing on her booty while she hit the blunt.

"I see you feeling better."

I laughed, and then put her on the counter and licked all over her neck. I thought she would stop me. Instead, she swallowed her glass of Henn and puffed on the blunt. Before she let out the smoke from her lungs, I put my mouth to hers and kissed her until the smoke entered my lungs. She placed the blunt in my mouth and took her pants off. I gripped her with my free hand until she stood on her tippy toes to get back on the counter.

I continued to pet her cat as I drank my liquor while she held the glass to my lips. Handing her the blunt back, she inhaled as I slid my fingers deep into her while twisting and turning my hand.

"Damn, you know I like that," she moaned.

So I went deeper, and eventually, those words got stuck in her throat and wrapped around a moan. "Who has been petting my cat?" I knew she hadn't been sleeping with anybody because I kept her too busy, and she was in her last year of college. She didn't have time to meet new people. I just wanted to hear her response.

"You know I don't have time to mess with nobody. I got a demanding boss."

As soon as those words shot out of her mouth, I went deeper, and she gushed all down my arm. I laid her back on the counter, making her hair rest in the sink. I licked every bit of her juices, and then ate her. She was shaking so badly that her knees clapped together like they were giving me a round of applause.

I stepped away from her to where I was completely out of the kitchen and told her to roll up. After the next blunt and three more major gushes, I called it quits, made her shower, and she went straight to sleep.

My nightmares were worse that night. That time, I was in jail for aiding and abetting Dre. I woke up in a cold sweat. Stephanie was already awake and getting things together for our trip to Nashville. I didn't want her to know about the dreams, so I rolled up and smoked the memories of the dream away.

Before hitting the interstate to face the three-hour drive to Nashville, we went to my condo. If I wouldn't have seen it with my own eyes, I wouldn't have known it was ever kicked in. It was just the way I left it yesterday morning except for the new door. I gave Tracey my house key just in case she had to leave; then we hit the interstate.

On the ride down to Nashville, I learned more about Stephanie than I had ever known. She had never been sexual with a man—not because she was a lesbian, but because she just never connected with a man long enough to sleep with him. She had dated many, but something had always prevented them from having sex. I told her, "It might just be meant for you to be with women or they weren't worthy to pet that monkey in between your legs." I laughed, and in the back of my mind, I was thinking the first man that gave her some dick would have her sprung.

She also told me that she had dated a soft stud in Nashville for a while. They would make trips back and forth to see each other, but after a while, the sex got boring, and she called it quits with the manly woman.

Stephanie told story after story, and I was glad she did because the ride to Nashville was the shortest I had ever experienced. The fact she drove 85 mph the entire time helped too. We made it downtown and parked. I asked her to stay by my side when she suggested waiting in the car for me.

When we walked in, the officer behind the counter checked us out. "How can I help you two ladies?" He was a young white officer with some of the prettiest blue-green eyes I had ever seen. He was tall, about six foot three, and nicely built.

"I need to speak with a detective about an incident that happened at my apartment in Bellevue."

He took down my name and address, and then walked toward the rear. When he came back he said, "You will be speaking with Detective Thomas. She's finishing up with another case and will be with you shortly." Shortly? I waited forty-five minutes before the detective called me back.

"Hello, Ms. James. I'm glad you were able to come in so we could talk face-to-face. Let me find somewhere we can talk." She shook and released my hand and escorted me down the blandest hallway I had ever seen. Maybe the dullness was supposed to put the person in question in an uneasy mood. That's probably why she wouldn't allow Stephanie to come back with me saying that we needed to speak in private. How private are you really, when you're being videotaped with someone watching live on the other end?

She recorded my story, asked a few questions, and then made me point out Dre in a picture lineup. There was a picture of Mike too, but I didn't point him out. Looking at the other three pictures, I assumed they were involved in some kind of way as well.

"That's him, that's Dre."

"Does Dre have any involvement in the sale or distribution of narcotics?"

"I don't know what he's involved in. Like I said, what he could do to me in bed was my only concern. He was a two-day, one-night stand. I didn't even know his full name until this."

Detective Thomas dismissed me, but I wanted to get confirmation that I wasn't in any trouble. I didn't want any more warranted searches or on the job pop-ups.

"Am I in any trouble?"

"No, Ms. James, you are not in any trouble, but if the suspect contacts you, please call me or the nonemergency police number." I assured her I would, and then left.

Chapter 6

All Gray Skies

We arrived at my Bellevue apartment, and shockingly, it was already cleaned. I was told my neighbors and maintenance men got together and cleaned it. Nothing was missing. In fact, they had left me flowers and a card expressing their sympathy for the way the police wrongly searched my apartment. Talk about kindhearted people. I hadn't even met those people, and they showed me kindness. That was what I loved most about the South. It was like having one big family. In California, I would have been robbed blind.

Everything was easy to pack up because it was neatly folded and organized. The women must have taken care of my clothing because my panties were folded and stacked in bunches by type, like thongs, G-strings, boy cut, etc. We packed up the apartment in less than two hours.

Stephanie cancelled the movers and rented a small moving van instead. She was sure we could handle it on our own. Once the van was loaded, I turned the keys into the front desk.

"Ms. James," the Hispanic pool man, who had never spoken to me before, called out to stop me as I walked out of the office.

I turned and addressed him. "Yes?"

He reached in his top shirt pocket and handed me a note. "Some guy told me to give you this. He was in the pool house with me while the police were searching your place."

I took the note from him and thanked him. Dre had slipped right under the cops' noses. He was better at hiding than I thought. I sat on the bench outside the office and read the letter:

Hey, Baby,

I'm sorry about your apartment. I'm watching them search through it now. I know you have a life somewhere else, but I want you to stay in touch with me. My full name is Andre Burns, and my birth date is 09/02/83. Just call the sheriff's department, and they will give you my booking information. I'm turning myself in Sunday night after I put my son to bed. Please don't be mad at me for all of this. I love you and fell in love with you after our first night together. There's something about you. I've never experienced this feeling before, and I ain't ready for it to stop yet.

—Dre

I don't know what happened but, after reading his letter, I felt sick to my stomach and ran to the office bathroom to vomit. With my face in the toilet, I kept seeing the words *I love you* in Dre's writing in my head. He didn't love me. He just needed someone to write over the next few years.

My mouth tasted like all the alcohol I had drunk the night before. I hate hangovers. Next, my head would be pounding. As a precaution, I took two Tylenol, extra strength, and then headed back outside to Stephanie.

"Girl, what did he say?"

I handed Stephanie the letter, scared that I would throw up again if I read it. "So, what are you going to do? He said it's love."

After all this time, she still didn't know me. I didn't give a damn what he called it. I would never be a drug-dealer's wife. Yes, I did feel something for him, but not love. Especially not in a week's time.

"I'm going to take this letter to Detective Thomas and be done with him and Tennessee."

We went to the police department. I did as I said I would, dropped my stuff off at the storage center, and then headed back to Stephanie's house to have a repeat of the previous night.

I got so drunk that I wasn't surprised when I woke up throwing up, especially after I saw Stephanie facedown in her bathtub.

"We can't hang," she said, trying to smile though it was visible she was sick to her stomach.

We ate Tylenol for breakfast and Pepto-Bismol for lunch. We didn't regain our appetite until around five o'clock when we decided to get something light, like a sandwich and soup, from the sub shop up the road.

"With everything going on with you this weekend, I forgot to tell you the good news, Savannah."

I stopped building my sandwich with the sandwich artist and looked Stephanie in the eyes. "Don't you fix your mouth to tell me we got the deal?"

She smiled and nodded her head yes.

We started screaming and jumping up and down. I even turned to the guy behind me in line and gave him a high five.

"They're giving us full control over all accounting in their West Coast markets. He said he was very impressed, and I sent him to Mr. Williams for the final contracting."

The news she gave me made everything I went through worth it. I would be promoted, and there might even be talk of me making partner. Stephanie would get a pay increase until she completed school and passed her exams. Then I'd hire her on as an accountant for our larger client base, since she had proved to be able to handle the job.

I was so excited about the news. When we got back to her place, I got my things ready for work, showered, and then hit the bed.

"No celebration sex?"

I didn't feel like it that night. What I really wanted was some dick. Before Dre, I hadn't had sex with a man for two months. My last sex partner was Amir, and that was a quickie because we were at the gym in the bathroom, trying not to get caught having sex in the one-person sauna. That might be why Dre's dick was so good to me. He was the first in sixty days to give me some.

"No, beautiful, not tonight. I don't think I could get in the mood if I wanted to. I just thought about Dre."

She looked a little disappointed, got in the bed, and asked me to hold her.

I held her through the night. Every time she rolled over, I adjusted myself in whatever position to keep her in my arms. That was the first night I didn't have a nightmare. Hell, I didn't have a dream at all.

I woke up to the sound of Stephanie's favorite morning show in the middle of the cohost reading a letter from an anonymous listener and giving them feedback on how they would personally handle the situation. I loved that morning show, but never had time to listen to it anymore. I wondered if the host's nephew still made his prank calls.

"Go shower. I made breakfast." She kissed my lips and walked back out.

After breakfast, we made our way to work. We were congratulated by our colleagues for closing the largest deal the company has ever had. Everything had been going good, and before I knew it, three weeks had flown by.

We had plans to go over the contract with our new client, Strax Industries, that morning, so I woke up two hours early and showered. I had recently installed a new showerhead where you can adjust the jets to the way you want it, and I loved the way the water was hitting my body. I had the temperature of the water just to my liking, nice and hot. The jets of water were hitting my nipples in a way that stimulated me.

As I rubbed over my body with my sponge, I stopped and squeezed my nipples slightly, turning them counterclockwise, and then back. I lifted my breast to my mouth and sucked on my nipple. Dropping my sponge, I slowly rubbed down my stomach to get in between my legs to my clit. I took a step backward, and the water was now hitting my lower stomach. Using my left hand, I put my left breast into my mouth and licked all over the nipple. My right hand was occupied with playing with my pearl tongue.

The feeling was getting good. I slid down the back of my shower wall until I felt the tub bottom under my butt. The water was now hitting me on the face and chest. I threw my leg over the tub's wall and scooted around the floor of the tub until I got the jets of water to hit me dead between my legs.

I started fucking myself with my fingers. Lying back and closing my eyes, I pretended I was being sexed wildly by an NBA player. I didn't have a player in mind because I couldn't concentrate long enough on anything but pleasuring myself. Whoever the hoop star was, he knew just how to handle me.

I kept fucking and stroking my pussy. I went faster with every beat of my heart. I felt it coming—oh yes—and I was exploding. I couldn't continue to fuck myself through the explosion in fear I'd black out due to the heat of the water filling my lungs with mist. I just lay back and enjoyed it. Thank you, Mr. NBA basketball player.

Starbucks was packed. I had never been there at 6:00 a.m., and after that day, I wouldn't be back that early again. I sat there and had my Frappuccino and Danish to get a look at the early birds in hopes of catching my next prey.

I didn't eat half of my Danish before it came back up. Rushing to the bathroom, I realized I'd been throwing up or waking up horny every morning for the last three weeks—and where in the fuck was my period? I'd had one two weeks before I met Dre. It'd been three weeks since the police raided my house, and that happened six days after I met him.

That made me two weeks late.

Me, pregnant? Hell, naw. I was on every type of birth control on the market. Somebody was getting sued if I was pregnant. I got a shot in my ass, swallowed pills daily, and practiced safe sex. That shit couldn't be real.

Dre must have gone inside me raw while I was asleep. Not only would I get a drive-by abortion, but a full STD screening. My gynecologist bill was going to be ridiculous because I wanted the works. I hoped I still had time to take the abortion pill. I couldn't stand to get another

DNC. The last one felt like someone ran in me with a train.

When I walked out of the bathroom, I sat down at the table to get myself together. I forced myself into believing the day would get better . . . but it didn't.

The meeting with Strax Industries was going well until we reached the terms of the deal. They agreed to give us 100 percent control of all accounts . . . as long as I was managing them.

On the upside of the deal, I would make partner at my accounting firm, be given a right in decision making since I would become the tie-breaking voter, have a projected $140,000-a-year salary before additional bonuses, and the best part, Williams and Williamson might have to change their name to Williams, Williamson, and James.

With figures thrown in your face like that, how could there be a downside? There is *always* a downside when getting or making money. That's where my "How much is it really worth?" rule kicks in. Never let the money be the decision maker. Think about what comes with making it. Will I have to work longer hours? Will I be in a safe environment? Will it shame my name or me? And how much ass will I have to kiss once I've accepted it?

This rule can be used when you're given money too. Does the giver expect something in return? If so, will I walk away with the respect and pride I had for myself before I accepted the money? And my favorite question again, how much ass will I have to kiss once I've accepted it?

In that situation, the downside would be more work and longer hours, but they would be the hours I decided I needed to give. I would have to manage a whole office of accountants and make decisions on what deals would make or break us if we accepted them. That didn't seem too bad. The part that was hard for me to stomach was moving back to California.

The office I would be presiding over was our California, downtown Los Angeles/Mid-Wilshire location. Mr. Nguyen, the owner of Strax Industries, said he would only be comfortable if I handled his account, and if I didn't, he would withdraw his offer.

I was shocked that I had impressed him so much. My goal was to get him as a client of our company, but the way he worded everything, he was becoming a client of mine.

"Ms. James, I will personally pay for your relocation, including shipping your belongings and vehicles. And don't worry about paying rent.

Wherever you decide to live, the bill is on us for the first three years, which should give you time to get settled into the new environment. I'll give you and your firm one year to get yourselves together to take over my workload while my current contract with my in-house accountant runs out. Again, we'd like to work with you. If your firm sends us anyone other than you as lead, we will take it as the agreement was breached, and we will not uphold our contractual obligations. Do you accept this offer in full?"

I needed time to think it over. Moving home was never a want of mine, and if anything went wrong, it would all fall on me.

"Can we plan to meet in a month so I can give it some thought? This is life changing and even though every inch of me is screaming yes, I'd like to give it some thought."

Everyone agreed, even Mr. Williamson, who looked disappointed when I made the request.

I felt like the HBIC (Head Bitch in Charge), and if I requested some time, then I would take some time, so his disappointed face meant shit to me.

Once the meeting was over, I went and told Stephanie what the offer was. No one in my office knew about my hate for my home state but her.

"Don't worry, Savannah, you'll get another $60 million-dollar deal . . . one day."

I didn't know if she was being sarcastic or really meant, "Bitch, you will *never* get a deal this big again. Pack up and move back to Cali," or if she was on my side and meant what she said. Either way, the decision was mine to make, and I had thirty-four days to decide by the date we arranged in the meeting. I was so stressed. I met Marcus at Houston's and smoked a blunt with him in the car.

"Aww, shit, what's wrong? Any other time I ask you to smoke with me, you are too busy to, so I know something's up." I hit his blunt two more times without answering him. He hit unlock on his door. "Follow me in your car. I'm going to park mine, and we gonna hit a bar."

I wasn't in the mood for a typical bar. I was stressed, horny, and hadn't had any dick in over a month. I had sex with Marcus a few times before, so I knew it wouldn't be a problem with getting him to fuck me that night.

I pretended to be ladylike about asking for some dick and suggested he follow me to the Renaissance on Peachtree because they had a bar. He knew what was up as soon as I made the suggestion.

"I'm going to make a stop, but I'm right behind you. Go get a room and have the drinks waiting on me." He handed me $300. "Text me the room number when you get it and take that blunt with you to smoke on the way. You know all of the hotels you like got a no smoking rule."

He was right. They did have a no smoking policy, and if he paid for the room, he would want us to stay all night. His sex was average to me. If I was going to get sexed well, it was going to be by somebody who knew what he was doing and somewhere I could smoke freely. Amir came to mind instantly. I needed some of his Jamaican loving.

I told Marcus I needed some time to find a place with smoking rooms and that I would call him later. If he was still available, we would meet up then.

I would use Marcus as my round-two dick, because Amir was a fifty-nine-minute man. Once he got his, he wasn't getting back up for a few hours. I could leave Amir and sleep with Marcus the rest of the night. I'd still be recovering from the beating Amir put on me, which would make Marcus's sex feel a lot better, and I would get the stamina Amir was missing with Marcus because his dick seemed to never go soft. Marcus popped X. I didn't know if he liked to be high or if it was his youngster version of Viagra, but both times I had sex with him, he had taken a pill first.

Amir said we would hook up around 8:00 p.m. at his place, so I texted Marcus and told him to meet me at the Hilton at 11:00 p.m. He agreed, and said he would bring liquor with him.

I waxed, then showered so I was as smooth as a baby's skin. I put on a red strapless dress that stopped three inches above my knees with matching pumps. Red lipstick was applied along with some red and gold dangling earrings.

My hairdo from the week before was still holding up. I let Jamie, my gay beautician, convince me to let it grow out. Now my two-inch haircut was a four-inch one, but I loved the new look. I thought maybe I should let it grow a few more inches and let Jamie work his magic.

I was looking and feeling good. I decided to leave my house at 7:00 p.m. Atlanta's traffic was horrible. That would allow me time to get to his place at 7:45 p.m. That meant I would be knocking at the door around 7:55 p.m.

After retouching my makeup and adding a little perfume just in case the humidity left a smell, I got out of the car.

Amir said he would be grabbing us something to eat from his family's restaurant and to have his cousin, who was also his roommate, let me in. When I knocked on the door, Ivan was there to open it. "Hey, now, look at you, looking all fancy and shit."

Ivan's English was a hundred times worse than Amir's was, and he was a hundred times sexier than Amir too. He was just learning English, and you could tell because everything he said involved a curse word.

"Dat motherfucker went to get you some food before he jukes you."

I wasn't going to listen to him, so I went and waited in Amir's room.

My phone rang, and a 615 number came up. Knowing it was Nashville's area code, I forwarded it to voice mail. Dre didn't have my new number, so who in the hell could be calling me from there? It rang again, and that time I answered. "Hello." There was a woman on the other end asking for me by my first and last name. "This is her."

The caller said she was calling from Nashville's Police Department. I got quiet. "Ms. James, we were calling to tell you that Andre Burns was arrested this morning and has cleared your name of all involvement. We will not be calling you again until he is released, so please keep your telephone number updated with us."

Dre's letter said he would turn himself in almost a month earlier. Yet he was *just* arrested?

"Hello, Ms. James, are you still there?"

I snapped out of it. "Where was Dre arrested?"

I could hear her typing. "Actually, he was found outside our precinct, sitting by the door and smoking a marijuana cigarette. His pockets were empty, and when the officer asked him what he was doing, he handed him his identification."

She chuckled like she thought Dre was stupid. I don't know why I felt the need to defend him, but I did. "Sounds like Dre made some arrangements before he turned himself in. It doesn't surprise me that your detectives couldn't find him. Hell, he watched as they raided my house looking for him, even though they never thought to search around the premises to see if he could have been hiding somewhere like the laundry room or pool house. Dre studied criminals and their ways of thinking before becoming one. I wouldn't be surprised if his case gets thrown out in court. It's really fucked up when the criminal is one of your own, isn't it?"

I could hear the irritation in her voice. "Is there anything else we can help you with?"

I replied, "No," and she ended the call.

"So, if Dre is your man, what da fuck you doing here?" By the language used, I knew it was Ivan, but, to my surprise, it was Amir. "You defend your man under *my* roof, while sitting on *my* bed, while he is on the way to jail?"

I stood up to get myself off this nigga's bed. "Dre is not my man, Amir." As soon as the words came out of my mouth, I realized Amir had just waved a red flag. He was jealous and questioned my other relationships with men. I'm sure he didn't think he was my only one. I continued. "And if he *was* my man, Amir, why would you care? We are just fuck friends, remember? You said you don't want a woman, that you like to be free, and I feel the same."

Amir went from mad to pissed. "In my country, men have many wives or sex partners, but a good woman sleeps with only one man unless she's a prostitute."

Hold the fuck up. Did he just call me a prostitute? "Well, I'm not your wife, and this isn't your country. Otherwise, you wouldn't need that green card. It's America, and I'm not a prostitute. I will continue to deal with other men until I'm married, and I don't foresee that happening."

He opened his door wider. "It won't happen. No man wants to marry a tainted woman. Get da fuck out!"

I grabbed my phone from his bed and walked out with my head high. On my way out the front door, his cousin looked at me while laughing. "I'll pay to juke that pussy, shit. See you later, prostitute."

I was so upset and hurt that I sat in my car and pulled myself together. "Marcus, you think you can meet me around 9:30 p.m. instead?"

He agreed. I rolled up another blunt, went, and got myself a three-piece chicken meal with coleslaw and mashed potatoes as my sides, and a sweet tea to drink. I sat in my car and ate.

Amir called me three times, but only left one message that said, "Savannah, I'm sorry I said those words to you. Please forgive me. I was going to ask you to be my woman tonight, and then I heard you on the telephone. If Dre is who you love, I do not compete, even if I am out on the streets while he rots behind bars. Please call back and let me know if you accept my deepest apology."

I laughed and continued eating my chicken. Amir and I would have had that argument anyway. I would have given him the same response when he asked me to be his woman. It was fate for us to go our separate ways that night and in that fashion. Who was I to stand in fate's way?

Chapter 7

Positively a Negative

Marcus was looking good when I pulled up to the hotel. I had never seen him dressed up, and I liked what I saw. He had on a blue and cream button-down, long sleeved Tommy shirt with khaki-colored pants to match. While we were away from each other, he went and got a fresh haircut, his face cleaned up, and he was wearing a very soft-smelling aftershave that wasn't harsh on the nose.

We checked in, and we then headed to the room. Once we arrived, he rolled up three blunts, and we smoked them back-to-back. He was drinking dark, and I just had Sprite. I wasn't in a drinking mood anymore. As soon as I felt high, I was ready to get the session started.

"I'll be right back, beautiful."

When Marcus went to the bathroom, I slid my dress over my head, then climbed on the bed in my bra and thong. I positioned myself so when he walked out, the first thing he would see was my legs spread apart and my finger rubbing my pearl tongue.

I had my knees apart, in a sitting position, with my pumps still on. I wanted him to taste me. I started rubbing my pearl tongue to imitate the stroke I wanted to feel from his tongue.

The toilet flushed, and I watched the door handle turn. I thought about moving my hand from my warmth so he wouldn't know I had been touching myself, but I changed my mind. We needed to be on the same page, and me stroking my pearl was the perfect indication of what I wanted.

"Keep going; I want to watch first, and then I'll show you how it's done." Marcus had never seemed to be the foreplay type, yet, I was feeling the freak he had in him. Although his request caught me off guard, I continued stroking my clit and with his hard dick in hand, Marcus watched the entire time.

"Let me help you out, baby." He came and put his tongue in the exact same spot my hand was in. It wasn't a competition. His tongue felt a hell of a lot better than my fingers. He was the winner—hands down. He licked me at a fast pace. His oral sex was wild. There wasn't a set direction he wanted to go in, and he covered them all. It was sloppy yet enjoyable.

I lifted my butt to bring it closer to his face. I had plans of slapping it against his tongue. Those plans were soon cancelled when he flipped me over to ride his face. There is nothing like a good rodeo. When it comes to riding a dick or a tongue, I'm game.

Marcus must have popped an X pill, because he placed both of his hands on each of my thighs and began lifting me up and down on his tongue. To regain balance, I placed both of my feet back on the bed and got into a squatting position over his face and rode his tongue.

I was getting a full workout. I could feel my thighs and calves tightening with every move. That's when the shaking started. I was coming in his mouth.

One good turn deserves another, so I fell into a sixty-nine position, placed his girth in my mouth, and started sucking him. I had never pleasured him with my mouth before. I don't know if I caught him off guard or if my head was just superb, but within the first minute, he sat up, removed it from of my mouth, and nutted on the bed.

Standing up, shaking, squeezing, and slightly pulling on his dick to get the remaining fluid out, he looked at me. "Savannah, your head is a killer. Girl, go bend over the desk. I got something for you." He grabbed his pants and pulled out the condom. I watched as he put it on. He was hard as steel, as if he hadn't exploded at all.

Apparently, I was moving too slow because he threw out the thought of me walking to the desk and bent me over the nightstand. He was in a zone. His eyes were rolling in the back of his head, and he kept licking his lips. Now I knew why he always sexed me with dark shades on. The light fucked with his eyes, and he wasn't able to control their movement on X.

He turned into a monster. I had to beg him to stop for a second to put the Gideon Bible away that he had my face lying on. I'm a cold-blooded sister, but I have boundaries. There will be no fucking on the good Word.

The sex hadn't changed since our last fuck. It was good, but it wasn't great. I had to mentally make myself come and, as usual, the man thought he did something because I came while he was inside of me. I hadn't been feeling like myself lately, so I let him believe whatever he wanted and promised to pretend to be sleepy as soon as he caught his next nut. Once he reached for another condom, I stopped him dead in his tracks.

"Marcus, baby, I can't take no more. Let me get a breather."

He smiled and walked toward the bathroom. "Okay, boo, I'm sorry—that's just the beast in me."

He closed the bathroom door behind him, and I bit my tongue to stop myself from hurting his feelings. Not like I cared, but I had already exchanged words with one man that night. I thought I'd take a break before my next confrontation.

Saturday was a much better day for me. I woke up with my period. Marcus might not have been a ten in my book, but his seven was enough to bring my period down. I was so happy I kissed his cheek on my way out the door.

The next three months had me so busy that I didn't have time to do anything but work. I had convinced Mr. Nguyen from Strax Industries that I needed more time to decide and, since we had a year to prepare, I would have an answer about moving to California within the next six months, of which I still had three remaining.

I hadn't had time to shop, have sex, or work out. I was horny, had gained at least twenty pounds that were visible in my butt and breasts, and I needed some clothes that fit. I had cancelled two gynecology appointments due to timing. Finally, I had time to go and get my STD scan. I was happy I didn't have to get a pregnancy test followed by an abortion. My period was back on track and coming like clockwork again. I had some bleeding at least once a month.

When I walked into Dr. Davis's office, I was surrounded by pregnant women. The women that weren't pregnant that were my age or younger, I tried to guess what they could be visiting for. There were a few teenage girls with their mothers. The ones who were smiling, I assumed, were there to get on birth control, and the ones who looked on the verge of tears were either pregnant, had an STD, or were there to see if they had been sexually active.

One of the girls sitting next to me tapped me on the shoulder to get my attention. "That lady over there wants you."

I turned to face a fifty-year-old white woman who was sitting next to a twenty-something, visibly pregnant woman. She must have been due any day. The lady who wanted my attention looked of age and wisdom. On her face was a freshly baked, homemade apple pie smile. "How many months are you, sweetheart? This is my eighth grandchild. I still can't believe the baby of my six children is about to be a mother."

I wasn't trying to be smart, but that was really rude of her to assume I was pregnant because I was a few pounds heavy. I rolled my eyes. "I'm not pregnant," I replied, and turned my back to her.

"I'm sorry, sweetie. I didn't mean to offend you. You're glowing. I just thought it looked like a pregnancy glow."

I cut her off. "Well, it's not."

Stephanie had told me the extra weight had me glowing the week before. Maybe the Shea butter was finally working.

When the nurse called me back, she asked me to pee in a cup and meet her in room seven when I was done. She took my weight, and I had gained twenty-five pounds in five months. I made a vow to work out as soon as I left.

"Ms. James, we have you scheduled for a full physical and STD screening, and a part of our screening is a questionnaire. You seem like you don't need help with it, so I'll leave you to complete it. I'll return in five minutes."

The questions on the form were so intimate. *How many sex partners had you had in the last twelve months?* I didn't have to think to answer that question. Going backward, it was Marcus, Stephanie, Dre, Amir, Gina, and the one-night stand I had with whatever his name was in New Orleans. Compared to the prior year, I had been a saint when it came to being sexual. I did a lot of traveling that year, which led to a lot of one-night stands.

I had gotten to the last question when the nurse returned. "Change into this gown and leave the front open." She scanned over my questionnaire, and I watched her eyes open wide, but she got herself together and played it off like it didn't happen.

"The doctor asked me to draw a little blood from you and send it to the lab so you can get all your results today like you requested." I extended my arm and turned my head. When she finished, she said, "I'll be back once Dr. Davis is done. We should be able to get you into ultrasound today. They are not that busy."

I guessed a full physical included an ultrasound of my uterus to check for cervical cancer. That was why I loved my GYN clinic. They were so thorough.

Dr. Davis was the sexiest female doctor I had ever seen. She was about forty years old, five foot eleven, about 155 pounds, and an ex-college basketball star with a gap between her two front teeth. But it was sexy on her oval face. She was a no-nonsense type of woman. She fussed me down the last time I got an abortion. She told me if I kept getting abortions that when I really wanted to have a baby, I wouldn't be able to have one. Silently, I prayed that would be the case so I wouldn't have to worry about taking care of anybody but me.

She walked in and greeted me with a smile. "How are you, Ms. James?" I greeted her back. "So, where do we begin? I made you my last patient for today since there is so much to do." She grabbed my chart and sat down looking over my questionnaire. "Four men, two women. Those numbers are down from last year," she said with a wink.

Thank God for the doctor/patient confidentiality. I could tell her anything, and if she exposed it without my consent, she could lose her license. She turned the page, read for a little bit, and stepped out of the room. She returned with the nurse. "I'm going to send you to get your ultrasound before I continue. That will allow time for your blood test to return. Daisy will take you to have it done, and I'll see you when you make it back."

That is why I would never get pregnant. The ultrasound technician put some kind of gooey, cold gel stuff on my stomach and pressed down on my stomach with her ultrasound instrument. To make matters worse, she stuck a probe into my vagina while I sat on my balled up fists. I love the word pussy, but the way that exam made me feel, "vagina" would be more suitable.

"Does everything look okay?" It was like I was talking to myself. The technician didn't respond. "Can you hear? I said, does everything look okay?"

She pulled the iPod headphone out of her ears. "I'm sorry. I'm not at liberty to say. The doctor will go over the results with you."

Daisy took me back upstairs to my room. I sat there for thirty minutes before Dr. Davis came back in with my labs and ultrasound results.

"Savannah, did you have a normal period last month?"

I nodded my head yes. "Why do you ask? Is something wrong?"

She asked the nurse to give us a minute. "I have not done your pelvic exam yet, but there are some things we need to talk about."

She moved closer to me. "Your urine test came back with high hCG levels, so I ordered the bloodwork, which confirmed my suspicions."

I didn't know what she was talking about, but my heart started beating fast. "What is hCG? Does it have anything to do with HIV or AIDS?"

She shook her head. "Your AIDS and HIV test came back negative, and you will be tested again in six months."

I felt the beating in my chest slow down.

"hCG is a hormone found in pregnant women. The blood test has confirmed your pregnancy."

She was wrong. "I've had a period for the last three months. They weren't normal periods, but I've been bleeding, and the last time I was sexual was over three months ago, with protection."

She held my hands. "You can still experience some bleeding early in a pregnancy. I'm sorry I have to be the one to tell you."

She didn't have to be sorry. I had a fix for it. "So, can you perform the abortion today?"

She looked at the ceiling, and then got out of her chair and walked to the desk where she set all of the papers. "You don't qualify for an abortion this time. By the results of the ultrasound, you are a week from six months pregnant. We have already determined the sex of the child."

It was a nightmare. Yes, I was awake, but I was in the middle of the worst nightmare I had ever had. Six months pregnant with Dre's baby, and I couldn't abort it. I felt my body hit the ground. When I woke up, I was in the maternity wing of the hospital all alone. I took all the monitors off my body. My door flew open, and Daisy came running in.

"Please put the monitors back on your stomach. We need to make sure your daughter is okay. You'll be released in the morning."

Her words meant shit to me so I continued to get up and get dressed.

"Ms. James, I cannot let you go until we are sure you and the baby will be okay."

That bitch must have thought it was negotiable. I walked past her like she was invisible. I made it all the way to my car without being stopped.

When I reached in my purse for my keys, they weren't there. I had emptied my purse on the back of the car when I was met by Dr. Davis.

"I have your keys and will give you time to get yourself together, but promise me you will not cause harm to you or the baby and that you will call me, because there are other options still out there for you." She handed me her cell phone number. "Call me when you're ready to talk. I don't care what hour of the night it is."

I snatched my keys and drove off.

Two weeks went by before I picked up the phone and called Dr. Davis. She scheduled an in-home visit with a planned pregnancy coordinator and me for that night at seven. When they arrived, I was eating a family-sized bag of Oreos with Doritos in the middle where the cream filling would be if I hadn't already eaten that part.

"Healthy snacks, Ms. James."

That was my first time meeting the woman and I already didn't like her. I rolled my eyes to express it.

Dr. Davis handed me the results from my STD screening that she had performed after I blacked out in her office. Everything looked good. Not even a yeast infection. My ultrasound results showed I had a few small cysts, which Dr. Davis told me was common in African American women my age and that we would check on them after I had my baby.

"Savannah, this is Margie Wright. She is our planned parenting coordinator, and I brought her along to give you some other options. I'm going to give you a checkup; then we all will talk. Lie back on your couch, please."

She pulled my shirt up to my breasts, and then tucked it under them. I watched her measure my belly with a tape measure, from my lower stomach to right below my heart. She requested I take my pants and panties off. She went deep inside of me with two fingers. That was the most penetration I had in months. I couldn't call anyone I knew for sex or that would make my pregnancy no longer a secret.

I wouldn't feel right going out trying to meet somebody new with a big-ass belly. I decided I would have to do my best with one of my sex toys.

She removed her gloves. "Margie, can you hand me the Doppler and the gel out of the warmer, please?" She covered my stomach in the gooey stuff again, but this time, it was warm. I heard static, and then a fast, swooshing sound. "That's the baby's heartbeat, and it sounds perfect."

The baby's heartbeat caught me off guard. It sounded so cute. I had started feeling the baby move a few days earlier. I could feel the baby go and rest on my bladder, which caused a lot of near accidents. I had to change underwear twice the day before.

Pregnancy is an amazing thing. I'd gone online to see what stage the baby was going through, and it almost brought me to tears. She was a little person. I even put my blunt out and stopped smoking weed because I read her lungs were the last organ to grow. I had made my decision before the doctor had arrived.

"Dr. Davis, I decided to give the baby to a foster care agency. I went online and looked some things up. I also made confidentiality contracts, which I would like both of you to sign. No one knows I'm pregnant but you and your hospital staff, and I want to keep it that way. I took off work for a few months to help a friend move and to start house hunting for a position I'm taking out of state, or so everyone thinks.

This will give me time to have the baby and send her off. I would like my entire chart and medical records once I am released from your care, and also any documentation that will link me to the child. I will also continue to be a patient of yours as long as you're a practicing physician. We will start all new records on my postpartum visit for your files.

"As for you, Mrs. Wright, I will need your help with placing my child in foster care because I don't want to meet with anyone face-to-face. I will set up video conferences so I can see the families and will supply you with a list of questions that I want asked. Dr. Davis, I am sure I'm making the right choice, but just in case I change my mind, I will have the foster care agency send updates to a PO Box every time my daughter is moved so if I ever want to regain custody, which I highly doubt, I will know where to start."

The two ladies looked at each other, and then Dr. Davis asked, "And what about delivery?"

I had that planned out too. "If my water should break unexpectedly, I will contact you or come to your hospital; otherwise, I want a planned C-section. From this point on, I would like house visits. I don't want to risk the chance of being seen."

I advised Margie that I would be doing all the work when it came to the agencies. All she had to do was oversee it and allow the video conferences to be set up at her facility, which she agreed with. Before they left, I got the signed copies of my confidentiality notices back and gave them unsigned copies. Nothing was left to do then but have the baby.

The next morning, I had Stephanie bring me all my files from work. She had no idea I was pregnant, and that was just how I wanted it. When she arrived, I was under a blanket on the couch. I told her I had the flu and would be working from home until I felt better and that I needed her to be my legs. She offered to come by and take care of me, but I lied and told her one of the women I was seeing had me covered and thanked her for caring. She stormed out of my house like lightning.

I was enjoying working from home. I didn't have to worry about how I looked, rush off to get my hair done, or have a set 8:00 to 5:00 to get the job done. I worked on my own schedule. I ordered everywhere that delivered for lunch, yet pizza seemed to be my favorite. I wondered if it was a food Dre liked because that was all I wanted. I'd call and order a vegetarian pizza, and then I'd say, add chicken. I could now eat two medium pizzas by myself.

I was getting big, but not just my waist and thighs. I could feel my breasts growing, and the implants were pushing more against my skin. My ass was huge, and no thanks to Amir's caveman dick. That time it was due to my little girl.

I worked from home for one month before I took three months off. I told everyone I would be between California and New York house hunting and helping my girlfriend from college get adjusted to her new home in the Big Apple.

Since I agreed to move to California, my job gave me more decision-making privileges now that I had made partner. The company name wasn't going to change, but everything else did. I also promoted Stephanie. She would be moving to California three months after me because of her graduation.

She would be my new lead accountant, grossing 70K in her first year out of college. Now that wasn't bad at all. With Mr. Nguyen paying for my relocation, it freed my money to help Stephanie with her move. I would aim to keep her somewhere close by my new home as long as her money permitted.

The videoconferencing was going well. There were four couples that caught my attention the most when it came to fostering my daughter. I had rules, strict rules, and most of the applicants didn't meet my criteria. Some of the applicants shouldn't be allowed to tend to children, in my opinion, like the Wests.

"We were really hoping to adopt a boy. We're old and manual will get harder over the years. Tending to our farm will become undoable and paying for someone else to do it is out of the question. If we had a boy, I could teach him what to do and eventually my great-grandfather's land would become his," Mr. West said matter-of-factly like he didn't just place a "help wanted ad" for child labor. I couldn't decide which one of us was worse—me for giving up the child to be burden free or him wanting one for free labor. Mr. West was the reason I made rules, and although they were blunt, they were honest.

Rule one, I would name the child, and the name could not be changed.

Rule two, I wanted my child to know she was in foster care as soon as she reached the age to understand it.

Rule three, the fostering parents would have to send updates, including pictures of my daughter, to the PO Box I would set up.

The final rule was that if I ever decided to come for my child, there couldn't be any hassle about me getting her back.

I reminded all the parents that I was a wealthy woman who was highly educated and stable. My only flaw was that I was missing the natural mothering gene. I knew I was no better than my mother was, but now I knew what my father meant when he quoted my mother: "Some things you will never understand."

The only difference between what I was doing to my child compared to what my mother did to us was that I wouldn't make the same mistake twice. That would be the only child I ever gave up, and that was a promise.

Chapter 8

Baby No Name

I had also composed a list of mandatory questions that had to be answered. It was my own application. I didn't give a fuck about them already being questioned by the agency. It was shit I needed to know.

One of the questions I had on my application was: Do both parents work, and if so, where? I needed to know that because I didn't want anyone taking her in as a foster child because of the money.

Another question was, where was your last vacation? I needed to make sure my baby saw the world. I didn't want her closed-minded or unaware of what was out there.

The most important question on my list was what their reason was for becoming a foster parent. I asked the question to see their facial expression. Fuck the words. I wanted to see who had it in their hearts.

My list was thirty questions long and, out of twenty-five couples from all over the United States, there were only four who answered all thirty to my liking.

The first couple was the Peters in Denver, Colorado. Both husband and wife were multiracial. Mrs. Peters was Asian and black, a junior high school history teacher, and Mr. Peters was black and white and worked construction for the state. I loved that they would teach my child diversity and the blindness of love. Love sees no color, race, or creed. I believe in that even if I personally didn't believe in falling in love.

When Margie asked the couple about their last vacation, both of their faces lit up like Christmas trees, and they began fumbling through their wallets, pulling out pictures. Mrs. Peters beat her husband to the punch.

"Our last vacation was to Disneyworld in Florida. We took our nieces to be princesses for the day." She held the picture up to the video camera, and there were two little girls, one dressed as Snow White, the other as Cinderella, with the castle behind them.

"We took the girls with us to Mt. Rushmore; they were bored clueless. This was our way of making up for it," Mr. Peters added, still smiling ear to ear.

My major concern with them was where they lived. I was from California and Dre was from the South. We were both from warm areas. I didn't want my child to be uncomfortable in Colorado's cold weather.

The next couple was the Jeffersons in Tacoma, Washington. They were an African American couple who owned a family restaurant that had been passed down three generations. What made them one of my top four was their answer to my question about their reason for becoming a foster parent. It wasn't Mr. Jefferson's teary eyes that touched me. It was his answer.

"I'm the third generation of Jeffersons to keep the family's restaurant alive. I'm almost forty-five years old, and the love of my life cannot carry my children. We have tried and tried, and I will not let my wife be hurt again by another miscarriage. I want to give her someone we can love as ours and be able to leave the family restaurant to. I don't care if it's a boy or girl. I want to leave it with my child. I do understand that you may decide to come back and take the child away from us, which would be heartbreaking and devastating, but I just want to see my wife in a motherly role. You will make my prayers and dreams come true."

They seemed like down-to-earth people who had been through a lot of heartbreak when it came to a child, and that was my concern with them. What if I did want my daughter back? I couldn't take another child away from them. They've already been hurt that way. I could be heartless at times and even cold-blooded, but to know I'll intentionally cause pain to someone whose only role in my life is helping me with my child was too much for me to sign up for.

The other two couples I picked lived in the South: the Greens from Baton Rouge, Louisiana, and the Hutchings from Savannah, Georgia. There wasn't anything spectacular about either couple. They just seemed like good-hearted people who knew there was more to the world than the South. They traveled frequently to those places, but they wouldn't call anywhere else home.

I had a hard decision to make and had less than a week to make it so whomever I chose could prepare for their new baby. I was leaving $5,000 at the hospital for the couple on a pre-paid card that I would load with money every now and then. On my daughter's tenth birthday, the card would become hers to use at her will.

I was nine-and-a-half months pregnant, two weeks away from my C-section, and still hadn't picked a couple. I would rewatch all the videos and go over all the answers and background checks again that night, and then make my decision the next day.

I was waiting on the pizza man to deliver my pizzas when I opened the door. Standing on the other side of my door was a skinny little white boy with an Atlanta Braves fitted hat on who looked like a hip-hop video dancer. I wouldn't have been surprised if he had broken out into a dance routine from one of Usher's videos.

"I got a certified letter for you." He looked down at my stomach. "Damn, you're due any day now, ain't cha? Yeah, you about nine months." Then he giggled like a geek.

I didn't know if he was asking or telling me. I snatched the letter out of his hand. There wasn't anything written on the envelope. "Who is this from?"

He moved over as the pizza man approached and headed back up the driveway. "Just read it. Bet you ordered everything on them pizzas too, ha-ha."

I went up the walkway to see what kind of car he came in. By the time I wobbled up the walkway, he was nowhere in sight. He must have run to the car just in case I came looking. I asked the pizza man if he had seen what kind of car the guy was in.

"He was standing by the big tree out front when I got out of the car, ma'am. He told me to follow him, and he would show me where you were. He started walking this way before I could catch up."

I paid the pizza man, thanked him for the little information he had given me, and walked back into the house. I had lost my appetite, or, should I say, put it on hold until after I read the letter. I threw the pizzas on the counter, and then made my way to the couch.

He wasn't a UPS or USPS worker. No one knew where I lived but a select few, who were Sandy, Stephanie, and her sister, Tracey. Marcus had delivered weed there before, but not to my door.

I paid my bills on time, and I wasn't in debt to anyone, and if there was someone out there I did owe, it wasn't bad enough for them to send a goon to my door. I made myself comfortable on the couch, then damn near had a heart attack. It was a letter from Dre.

Ms. Savannah James,
You're a hard woman to track down. Did you really think I wouldn't keep up with you? I ran your license plate before I came by your house

that Friday night. You rolled up on my boy at the gas station in a brand-new car, asked for some green like you knew him, pulled up with out-of-state plates, bought an ounce, then called me to deliver another one somewhere in Bellevue that same night. Hell, yeah, I had you checked out. I thought you would have known better. I told you I graduated with a master's degree in criminal justice (sorry I left the "master's" part off originally). I know my shit, and what I don't know, I have detectives for friends to teach me. You're probably thinking if I know so many people, why am I in jail? Let's just say I was warned they was coming, but disappearing would have made shit worse for me and drawn attention to my friends. I had given up on you when I found out you changed your number to get rid of me. Yeah, the police told me you didn't want to be bothered with me and that you turned in my last letter.

For some reason, I don't think you're going to turn this one in though. I couldn't get yo' ass off my mind for shit, so I sent my nigga by your spot in Atlanta. When he got there, you were dressed up all sexy and shit. I got jealous and told him to follow you. Yo' ass went to a nigga's house, and again, I was done with you.

You know what's funny? I started feeling sick over you, so I thought I'd give it one more try 'cause I knew then I really was in love with you, but my boy said you don't ever leave the house, your car is parked dirty as hell, and your mailbox is full. You know how to play gone good.

Let me tell you how I found out you were home or where you fucked-up your game of hide-and-go-seek. Every time my boy would fall through, you was ordering pizza and shit. You can't deliver food to a house where no one is home, can you? So he paid the delivery boy to deliver your chicken pizza with everything on it last month, and guess what he told me? Savannah is pregnant! I asked him if he was sure, and he said positive unless you swallowed a whole watermelon. My only question for you is, when are you having my baby? I know you think you're smart and will probably lie and say it ain't mines, and that's cool. More power to you. I know I ain't the kind of nigga you planned on having a baby by with your exquisite lifestyle and all. But you still should have let a nigga know.

So what do you and your rich friends do? Travel through the hood looking for some thug dick 'cause all them tight shirt, tie-wearing-ass niggas ain't fucking you right? I can't do

shit while I'm in here but count these eighteen months down to my freedom. I guess we will have to talk later about it, huh?
  —Dre
  P.S. Chicken pizza with all the toppings is the only way I eat my pizza. I don't eat pork. You see, Savannah, no matter how hard you're trying to keep me out of my child's life, it's still a daddy's baby.

I put the letter down and felt the water fall down my legs. I was in labor. I called Dr. Davis and told her to meet me at the hospital. It was time. I grabbed the bag I had packed, put Dre's letter in it, and drove all the way to the hospital in the worst pain I had ever felt in my life. I turned on the radio to try to comfort myself, and Sade's new song about being a soldier was playing. I toughened up and made the drive.

Dr. Davis and two men were waiting on me with a wheelchair when I pulled up at the emergency room. Once I sat in the chair, everything else went quickly. I was pushed in a room, put on a table, Dr. Davis stuck her hand between my thighs, her gloves came out red, she hit a button on my bed and said, "stat," and the nurses ran in. I lay back and after two pushes, the baby was out and screaming.

She was eight pounds, two ounces, nineteen inches long, and she was the prettiest little girl I had ever laid eyes on. "She looks just like you," Dr. Davis said while bringing her over to me.

I thought to myself, she has never seen Dre. She looked like her father and me combined. Her skin was lighter than the both of ours. I guess her color would come with time.

"Would you like to hold her, Savannah?"

Previously I had said I didn't want to see or touch the baby once she was born, but I nodded my head yes.

The baby was crying when the doctor handed her to me. She soon stopped as if she knew who I was. I had read online that babies had a sense of knowing things and that it was good to talk to them while they were in your stomach so they could get familiar with your voice, and I did just that.

There was no one around me for three months. I had to find a way to hear my own voice, so I talked to her and read her a book of my choice. I tried reading her children's stories, but they were too fictional. I wanted my daughter to know what was really on the other side of my stomach. We ended up reading *The Coldest Winter Ever* by Sister Souljah.

I know there is a lot of adult content in the book, but there were so many lessons she could learn to help her become a better woman. That's why it was my first choice. I packed the book in my hospital bag and wrote her a message in it that I would give to her new parents to give to her once she was old enough.

As I said earlier, I didn't have anyone positive in my life while growing up. I wish someone had handed me Sister Souljah's book. I might have made better life choices.

The nurses pushed me into my room while they ran the normal tests on my daughter. "Get some rest, Ms. James. We will keep her in the nursery with us tonight."

I didn't need any rest. Hell, I had a lot to do in the next three days. "When you're done with your tests, bring my daughter back, please. Thank you. And can you pull that curtain and close my door?"

As soon as I pulled out my laptop, there was a knock on the door. Dr. Davis and Margie had come to me with updates.

Margie spoke first. "We have requested her Social Security card to be sent here so we can give it to the parents. They will be coming shortly to do her birth certificate, which you said you did want to complete with your information. What is the child's name?"

I named my daughter on the ride to the hospital. "Her name is Sade Chrisett, and she will have her father's last name, Burns." I waited for a response, and I knew Dr. Davis would have one.

"Did you decide to give her father custody? If not, which couple will it be? We need to notify them that the child has been born."

I was hearing her talk, but I wasn't listening. My mind was spinning around. Not only did I just have Dre's baby, but also he knew I was having her. I needed my baby to go as far away from him as possible.

"No, she will not be going with her father, and if I didn't like you, Doc, we would be having words. I have chosen the Jeffersons to raise my child." I knew I would be breaking their hearts if I ever decided to take her from them, but hell, she was my child, and we could come to an agreement on something.

Margie walked out the door in a hurry. I guess I pissed her off. I was back to me now . . . Fuck her and what she thought was best. If the bitch walked a day in my shoes, she would have corns.

For the last two weeks, I'd been thinking of ways to better myself, looking back on my mistakes. I'd made plans to have my shit back tight. The move back to California was going to be a good thing after all. I could get revenge on everyone I needed to pay back, show off the new Savannah James, and make lots of money while doing it. But, first things first.

I needed to wrap up things in the South. I would be released from the hospital the next night, and Sade would be headed to Washington the day after. Once she was out of the South and untraceable, I would send her daddy a letter and make sure it was one he wouldn't forget.

I called my uncle Johnny, who was now coaching at UCLA. "Hi, Uncle Stranger."

He cleared his voice. "Is this my baby girl?" After all this time, he had no kids and still treated me like I was his.

"Who else would it be? Uncle, I need your help with something. Do you have a minute?" I told him about my promotion to partner and that I would be moving home. I asked if he could start looking for a house or condo by the beach since UCLA was right down the street.

"Baby, them places is high out there. Why don't you move out here to Torrance or Carson by me? You could own a house for the amount you're going to pay in rent living by the water."

I knew he would want me near him, but living near him would not impress anybody. I wanted to break hearts. "Uncle, I am way above those areas. Yes, they are nice, don't get me wrong. With my income, however, I want the best. I don't want to spend my money on security."

He took a deep breath. "Savannah, you ain't got to impress nobody, baby. Everybody from the old neighborhood is still in the old neighborhood. You and Keisha's little sister are the only two who made it out."

He didn't understand all the hell I went through. "I don't give a damn what they are still doing. I already know I'm better than them. I just don't like being around broke, goalless people. Uncle, you should understand. You made it out too."

I had forgotten I cursed. "You better watch your mouth. What has gotten into you? I'll find you a place in Malibu, Pacific Coast Highway, or Rodeo Drive if that's what you want. You got 90210 money. You want me to look there too? What I'm trying to get you to understand is it doesn't matter where you lay your head if your shit stank. Putting it in a fancy box just presents it better. I hope this move is going to be a good thing for you. Have you told your father yet?"

Always the voice of reason. That time I wasn't hearing it. Trying to stand in my way would be like jumping in front of a train. I wasn't going to stop until I ran your ass over. "I'm sorry for cursing, and, no, I haven't talked to him yet. I'm going to call him next. And thank you, Uncle. Any of those places you named will be fine. I would like to move in by next month, so move fast. How much do I owe you?"

There was silence, and then he said, "Money can't buy love, baby. I will find you a place this week and e-mail you the details. I love you with your hardheaded ass. You got to learn everything the hard way, don't you? Why do you think you didn't get that scholarship to USC? 'Cause of your attitude. I'm getting off this phone. Good night."

He hung up before I could say thank you back. My next call was to my daddy. "Hey, Daddy." He must have been smoking a cigarette because I could hear the lighter flickering in the background.

"Hey, baby, what's new?" He always asked me what was new like he was waiting on some exciting news. It felt good to be able to give him some.

"Daddy, I got promoted at work and will be moving back to California to run my own branch of my company."

He was so excited. I asked him to set up a PO Box in his name the next day, but he needed to set it up at the twenty-four-hour post office in

Hollywood. I told him it would be my business PO Box, and I would be the only one permitted in it. We talked for an hour about my new position and me. He was proud of me and made sure he told me every chance he got.

"Savannah, you have come a long ways, baby. I'm so proud of you. I wish your mother could see what a beautiful and successful woman you have become."

I hated when he brought her up, so I rushed off the phone saying I had to make more phone calls and that I would call him to give him my new address as soon as Uncle Johnny found me a place.

Before I could call Stephanie to tell her I would be back the next week, the nurse brought Sade back in the room. I fed her, changed her, and then told her my game plan. I told her I loved her and would be supporting her throughout her life even if she never saw me again. I spoke to her like I was speaking to an adult. There was no goo-goo and ga-ga in my voice. I gave it to her straight.

"I never wanted to have a child, Sade, but then you came along. I have to be honest, if I would have had the opportunity to abort you, I would have, but it was too late. I love you and will always love you. You're the only thing in this world that is mine. I can't mother you and teach you to be a woman. I barely could teach myself to be one, and I'm still learning. I want you to feel the love of two parents, something I never had and don't think I can give. If you grow up to hate me, I will understand. But, like the bitch that left me said, 'some things you will never understand.'"

I must really be the coldhearted bitch everyone called me because I wasn't sad at all when I told her good-bye the next night. I took a hundred pictures of her with my camera phone and kissed her good-bye.

The next day at that time, she would be arriving in Washington to her new mother and father and I would be writing her sperm donor a letter he would never forget.

I headed straight to Marcus when I left the hospital and got some weed. He commented on my weight gain, saying I looked thick. If he only knew.

Just in case Dre had his goons spying on my place, I went and stayed at the Residence Inn in Gwinnett for a week. I stopped at TJ Maxx and grabbed a few outfits, some underwear, two work suits, and some comfortable shoes. Once I made it to the Residence Inn, I didn't leave, and there really was no need to. There was a laundry room, workout room, outdoor pool, and a minimarket inside. The hotel was made like a small condo so it had an at-home feel.

My first day there I slept the entire day. I didn't realize I was that tired until I woke up at four o'clock the next afternoon. I walked over to the desk, grabbed my notebook, and started writing Dre.

I wrote his name on top. This wasn't an average nigga I was dealing with, so I tried to use some of the business law I learned while in college mixed with the hood, criminal shit I learned in Los Angeles. I had to be careful about what I wrote, because any errors I made would be like leaving him clues. This time when I left Dre, he would fully understand that I meant it, or he would be hunting me down . . .

Mr. Andre Burns,

How are you? Don't worry about writing me back to tell me because I really don't care. I've heard of women being sprung over dick, but never the other way around. I wonder if it was the way I fucked or sucked you that has you stalking me. You win the best detective of the year award. I did think if I changed my number and terminated my lease, I would be cutting off all ties with you, but I see I was wrong.

There are some things you are right about; your intelligence has shocked me. You were right about me not giving the letter you wrote me to the police. With all of your connects on the judicial side, I would be wasting my time, and I am not a snitch. I gave Nashville police the letter to buy you time. I was thinking they would hunt down someone else if they saw you had a date for when you were going to turn yourself in. This was a lie, and now I realize you used me as bait. You wanted me to give the police the fake date so you could make other arrangements. You have a full understanding of the law, I see. To address what you wrote in your letter about being in love with me, all I can say is, you know like I know, it wasn't love. We just have a lot in common and some beautiful sex.

I'm not ashamed to say the dick was good. I just wish it was connected to a better person, or at least a man who was worth my time. Maybe if you weren't such a criminal we could have had more, but sorry-ass niggas like you don't change. I won't waste this letter bad-talking you and telling you that you ain't shit; you already know that. What I will tell you is that you were right about me being pregnant by you.

You were also right about me not wanting you in our daughter's life. And by the way, that was smooth how you had your friend deliver my pizza to get a status on me. Hats off to you.

Now that I told you everything you were right about, let me tell you where you are wrong. You were wrong to think that I went into hiding to stop you from knowing I was pregnant. I went into hiding to stop the world from knowing I was pregnant.

I am not a caring person. My only concern is me and what's best for me. Your beautiful eight-pound daughter, who looked just like you, will never know either one of us. I hired an out-of-country adoption agency to ship her off to her new parents two days after she was born.

I know you don't believe me and will play detective again, and that's fine, but the next time one of your goons finds me, they will see me alone without a child. I have destroyed all the records of the birth and my pregnancy to prevent you from trying to get her.

You told me how you would have tried to get custody of your son, so I had to make sure I didn't leave you the option of getting her. If you still don't understand what I'm saying to you yet, let me make it simple.

I am well paid and only use men for sex. Fuck a relationship, love, marriage, the white picket fence, and fuck the dog too. That shit ain't for me, and neither are you or your child.

So have a nice life, Dre, and remember not to drop the soap.

—Savannah

P.S. The next time you want to find me, you should knock on my door yourself. Don't send someone to handle your business. When and if you do come knocking, I'll be waiting.

Chapter 9

Can't Dwell on the Past

"Fuck fuck fuck!" Tyrone sent me on a trip down memory lane. It had been two years and ten months since I had given birth to Sade. I hadn't changed my mind about giving her away. I loved having my freedom, and she would have stopped that.

The first few weeks I had nightmares about Dre finding her and raising her, but they soon stopped. I checked the PO Box for updates every two months and loaded money on the card once a month.

Sade was beautiful. She had long, pretty hair now with her daddy's lips. She was going to be a heartbreaker. I just hoped she wasn't as hot in the ass as I was.

If anyone in Washington had known Dre, they would be able to look at her and tell she was his. I'm not going to pretend like I thought about her a lot over the years, as running a company kept all my attention. I barely had time for sex. I had fucked only four people over the last two years, and three of the four of them were one-night stands.

I managed to sleep with Devin once a month because he worked in the building next to mine, so getting a room for lunch instead of eating came easy. Even my revenge plan had been put on the back burner until just recently.

Whenever I visited my daddy, there was never anyone from my past around. I saw lazy-ass Memphis, who was still selling drugs even though that line of work had gotten him shot. What a stupid motherfucker. You have been arrested and shot over the shit, yet you are still out there all day and night. You deserve every-thing that comes your way if you're that dumb.

So what if he was my brother? I was glad I didn't inherit the idiot gene he had gotten from my mother. "The love for money, but getting it in all the wrong ways." I worked hard for mine.

I realized I always decided to visit Monday through Friday, so I decided to pop up on a Saturday, which turned out to be in my favor. When I pulled up to my daddy's house, Keisha and Christina were about to pull off. If it weren't for the ho in them, I would have watched them drive off. Instead, they stalled to see who was driving the pearl-colored Charger with the pearl tint. Not like they knew my Charger was previously black, but I changed my paint and license plate to make it harder for Dre to find me, so my car looked brand new.

I rolled down my window. "What's up, Keisha?"

She pulled over, parked, and then ran up to me. "Damn, Na-Na, it's been years. Look at you, girl, you are beautiful."

I quickly corrected her on the name. "It's Savannah. I don't go by Na-Na anymore." I mustered a fake smile.

I really wish I could have told her she was looking good too, but it would have been a bold-faced lie. She and Christina looked mid- to late forties. They had a drained look about them. I guess all that fucking, abortions, drinking, and weed smoking had finally caught up with them.

"Excuse me, Savannah. How are you doing? We need to catch up. Last I heard you had graduated with a master's degree in something and was running Atlanta. Let me borrow something." This bitch still talked like she was seventeen years old.

"Yes, I graduated with a master's in business and accounting, but I've been in California for two years now. I have my own firm here and you're in a new Malibu. You don't need any handouts from me."

She laughed. "Girl, this is my baby daddy's car. You know I had a baby by fine-ass Tyrone from the park, right? Girl, you should come to the barbeque. I know everybody wants to see you. And we can catch up."

I was looking my best. I went and got my hair and nails done that morning. It was now shoulder-length and cut into layers. I was wearing bright orange BCBG sandals with a matching bag. It was midsummer. My jean skirt was an extra mini one with a form-fitting shirt that cuffed my breasts. Since the birth of Sade, I had lost fifty pounds and was now 160 pounds.

"Is it at the park down the street?"

Christina felt the need to answer. "Yep, and it started about an hour ago. They playing basketball out there. You might want to change your clothes. I know you want to play." Both of these young-minded, old-looking bitches laughed.

"No, I don't play anymore, but I'd love to come. I'm going to run and say hi to my daddy; then I'll be on my way."

Christina looked at me like I was stupid. "Memphis and your daddy went up there thirty minutes ago. When Keisha said everybody was going to be there, she meant it. The only person who ain't going to be there is her little sister's smart-ass. She's off at college."

Everybody kept saying, "You and Keisha's little sister." Hell, I don't even remember Keisha having a little sister. Whoever she was, I was proud she made it away from here.

I jumped in my car and followed them to the park. The street was packed with hood-rich cars. There were a few Malibus, Caprices, Impalas, and Monte Carlos. When I pulled up, everybody turned around to see who was behind the tint.

I quickly applied an extra layer of lip gloss, got out of the car, and walked to the table my daddy was seated at.

"Savannah, baby, what you doing here? Come sit down." That man kept a cigarette in his mouth.

"I was coming to visit you when Keisha and the girls invited me here. I think I'm going to say hello to a few people before I sit, Daddy. I'll be back."

I headed straight to Keisha, Christina, and Melinda, who were sitting in the middle of everything to keep all the attention on them, as usual. As a teenager, I hated them for always having to be the center of attention, but as an adult, it was just what I needed. My goal for the day was to make every man there want me more than they ever wanted Keisha, and this included Keisha's, Melinda's, and Christina's men.

"Savannah, what do you do for a living?" Melinda asked, genuinely looking interested, but she was cut off by Christina's no-class-having ass.

"Fuck that, we want to know how much you making, rolling up on us in your new Charger and shit with your expensive-ass clothes."

Her comment was an indication that she and Keisha had a conversation about me on their way to the park. Normally, I wouldn't answer that question, but everyone was around. "Just a little over 140K a year, after taxes."

The bitch kept coming with the questions. "So you paid to deck your daddy's house out, huh? It wasn't the insurance money he got when your granny died, because Memphis didn't get shit."

My daddy told me Memphis had dated her. What in the fuck was he thinking even mentioning to her that my daddy was receiving a check for his mother passing?

"Yes, I couldn't convince him to move away from here, so I thought I'd make him a little more comfortable."

I excused myself because Stephanie was calling. That was the break I needed from all of Christina's nosy-ass questions. I had actually forwarded Stephanie's call to my voice mail and turned my ringer off so I could pretend like I was in conversation, but I really listened to the conversation they were having at the table.

"I think she's still a lesbo. Where's her man or her kids? The bitch is almost thirty. She's making all that money with nobody to spend it on but her daddy. Something about that picture ain't right."

Listening to Keisha talk, I knew I would have to snap on one of them before today was up, and I would need to do it publicly. Christina would be my victim because I heard her volunteer to question my sexuality for Keisha.

She waited until Tyrone and the fellas were playing basketball to question me. I stood by the baseline, watching the half court three-on-three game.

Three out of the six men on the court belonged to one of them, or at least was their baby's daddy. Tyrone was Keisha's, Javier was Christina's, and Anthony, known as Big Ant, was Melinda's.

"Girl, you still love basketball. Does your man play? Or does your woman play?"

There was a roar of laughter. They even called time-out on the court to laugh at Christina's attempt of calling me out.

"No, you ignorant bitch, I played. If you could get dick off your mind long enough, you would remember that. To answer your question, no, I don't fuck women anymore. I take my dicks long and hard. Unlike you, I'm choosy about who I will have a child by, and I don't want kids. I don't want marriage, either. All I want is a good fuck every now and then by a nigga who knows what he's doing. Now if that was your attempt of trying to get at me, I don't let women eat my pussy anymore, so, sorry."

Keisha moved away from her and stood next to me. "Christina, you stupid for asking Na-Na . . . sorry, I meant Savannah, that. She is grown and on her shit. Don't bring up her past."

I took a step away from Keisha and said, "Anything you think you know about me or remember about me, you can throw it out. I've been gone over ten years, and a lot has changed."

I then turned to the fellas after deciding Javier, Christina's baby daddy, was going to be my first victim. "Keep playing, y'all, I've missed seeing y'all play. That college shit was okay. But it ain't nothing like seeing some real niggas hoop." I licked my lips at Javier so he would know what was up, and Big Ant smiled.

"Damn, girl, you came home country as fuck, but welcome back."

I left the cookout with everyone's respect and everybody's telephone number.

***

Keisha called so we could go to the nail shop two weeks later. I treated her to my salon because all she had budgeted for our trip was forty dollars, which was only a polish change at my shop.

She talked about her and Tyrone the whole time we were being pampered. She did admit they weren't in a relationship, but you couldn't tell they weren't with the way she was checking his voice mails.

"I stole his password and been checking his shit ever since. I know he's fucking other bitches. I'd just like to know who."

That was the craziest shit I had heard in a long time, but to the average hood bitch, it was normal. Once you had a baby by someone down there, you had ownership of their sex organs. Men felt like their baby mama's pussy was always theirs, and women felt like they owned the dick.

I wasn't enjoying her company at all. I just needed information from the horse's mouth so I could know how to attack them where it would hurt most. Keisha attempted to apologize again for Christina questioning my sexuality.

"You know that bitch can't control her mouth. Between you and me, she and Melinda are both bisexual. They have threesomes together and with other bitches."

Being two-faced was one of Keisha's best qualities. Later that day, she would be bad-mouthing me to the same people she was talking about now. It was her own circle of life.

"Keisha, I am not worried about Christina. She was and still is a nothing-ass bitch to me. I could buy, sell, and trade her ass on eBay, but I would be wasting my time. She is like soiled laundry. Once it gets that mildew smell, there is nothing left to do but throw it away or tear it into rags." I didn't hate her enough to dispose of her, but I would tear her apart.

"Well, that bitch in jail for the next two weeks. She had to turn herself in for not appearing on some traffic ticket she got."

Thank you, big mouth. That was the information I wanted. I texted Javier and asked if he could join me for dinner while sitting with Keisha. I had him meet me at the restaurant at the end of the Santa Monica pier and, of course, he agreed.

Javier was Mexican, zero percent black, but he carried himself like a black man. He kept his long hair cornrowed to the back, had a goatee that reminded me of a rougher Jon B, and his voice had no traces of an accent.

He was one of the guys who paid me no attention on our basketball team when we were younger. I won the point guard position over him, and that was all she wrote. Even when I made the final point that won us the championship game in overtime, he celebrated with everybody *but* me.

Having sex with him at the end of the night was going to take everything in me, but it must be done. After we ate, I invited him back to my time-share property off Pacific Coast Highway just to smoke and continue the conversation.

"Damn, Savannah, this yo' spot?" He looked around at my paintings and statues and didn't dare touch anything, as if he was nervous he would break something.

"Yes, this is one of my places. I rent it out to other people when I'm not in it, but everything here is mine. I rent it as a furnished vacation spot. No one can rent it longer than two weeks." I handed him the weed and asked him to roll up three blunts while I showered.

"I still can't wait to see you smoke. You're so different now. You don't look like the type to smoke."

I smiled, and then headed to the bathroom. I had stopped and gotten a new matching zebra print panty and bra set on my way home. I wrapped myself in my robe and the zebra prints and sat next to him on the couch. We smoked blunt one. I was back in Cali, so the weed was good and worked immediately.

"Javier, I want to do something to you and with you that I haven't done since I've moved from the South, but I want it to be between us. No one can know about tonight. Christina and I are friends, but I can't help it that she decided to have a baby by the nigga I've always wanted to be with. I just don't want the wrong person to find out and it get back to her. Like you heard me say at the park, I don't want anything from you but sex. I do appreciate you paying for the meal, but it wasn't necessary for what I want. So, can you handle keeping a secret with me? Not even your boys can know."

He kept smoking the blunt.

I removed my robe, stood in front of him, and snatched the blunt out of his mouth. I hit it twice, and then got on my knees. "You haven't answered yet, Javier. Do you disagree?"

He mumbled, "No."

I stood up and led him to my bedroom. He undressed without me asking. While he was undressing, I hit record on my surveillance camera, and then lay on the bed.

"You sure you want to fuck me, Javier? What about Christina?"

He laid me back on the bed. "Fuck, Christina. She just my baby mama. I don't give a fuck about her. Can I lick that pussy?"

I agreed and spread my legs. His head was on point. There was no sucking involved. He licked my pearl tongue about 200 times in a minute.

When he was done, he kissed my body from my pearl tongue to my belly button, and then licked me from my belly button to my nipples. I reached under my pillow and handed him a condom. I didn't get to look at the size of his dick, but by the feel, he had about seven inches to give.

His stroke was slow and deep. He kissed me all over my neck with every stroke. Once thirty minutes went by, I had enough of his slow pace and decided to speed things up. Javier hesitated to get on his back, which let me know that was his weak spot and he would more than likely nut soon, which was fine with me.

To get full revenge, I had to treat it like a full-time job and not look for pleasure. I sat on his dick and moved as fast up and down as I could. That was the first time in my life I heard him speak Spanish. He yelled, *"Ooooooo, Dios mio,"* which meant "oh my God," and then he nutted.

As he went to wash up in my bathroom, I hit stop on the video. I had gotten all the footage of Christina's baby daddy that I needed.

When he was done, he attempted to get back in the bed with me. That's when I reminded him of our agreement.

"No, Javier, it's time for you to go, baby. Remember what I said. All I want from you is sex. Maybe we can do it again another day if you want."

He looked disappointed but agreed. That was one down and two to go.

When I went to work Monday, Stephanie had good news for me. She had signed us up for an intern program with the California State University, Northridge, otherwise known as CSUN. This would allow undergrads the opportunity to get real-world work experience while giving us a few hours of unpaid labor.

The first two interns would be arriving next week and would be working twenty hours a week for two months. At the end of their stay, we would type letters of recommendation and send them away with a thank-you check. This was Stephanie's idea.

She handed me both of their background checks. I didn't read them over besides their names, Erika Soto and Brian Hasty. I made two employee folders for them and locked them in my file cabinet.

This was Stephanie's first senior accountant project that she was fully in charge of. I
advised all three of my senior accountants that I
expected one project that bettered or gave back
to the community or young kids a year, and this
was Stephanie's.

Robin Dyer had suggested we adopt a youth
baseball team who we would sponsor by purchasing all the equipment they needed. I agreed
to it, and now we have a first-place trophy and
team picture in our lobby.

Zach Markova, my other senior, suggested
we feed the homeless during Thanksgiving,
and that worked well too. We set up tables and
chairs at the Los Angeles mission and fed about
800 people. Yes, it was more expensive than
sponsoring a team, but we could write it off
during tax time as charitable contributions.

Stephanie's was the first cost-free idea that
allowed everyone to win. The school could continue providing an internship, the students
could gain on-the-job experience, and we gained
free laborers. Stephanie was still my full-time
secretary. Getting an intern to do her secretarial
work would be a pleasure for her.

I knew she hated working both jobs, but there
was no one else qualified to handle my things
but her. She handled both my business and

personal affairs. She had even scheduled a trip for me and Big Ant to Las Vegas for the weekend in two weeks.

I knew Ant liked to shoot dice. I had her call and tell him I wanted to go to Vegas and I didn't want to be alone. She asked if he would join me. He answered yes; then she transferred him to me.

"This is Savannah," I said, when I answered the call.

"Hey, you had your secretary set up a gambling trip for us?"

Trying to sound believable, I replied, "Yes, Anthony. I'm still adjusting to being home and wanted to go to Vegas. Keisha and the girls are not up to speed when it comes to shooting dice, and you're the only person I know who would make a great gambling mate. Plus, I was hoping to catch up with you in private. No one would have to know about our little trip but us. As a matter of fact, with you having a child by Melinda, that may be the best way to keep it—just between you and me."

There was a time when we were younger when I had written Big Ant a letter telling him I liked him. He had turned me down because I was Memphis's little sister, and they were best friends. The years had destroyed their friendship. My father told me Ant and Memphis had gone as far as fighting in the backyard a few years back, so he should have no reason to turn me down now.

"Yeah, Savannah, that's cool, and it would be best if we kept it between us. You know how Melinda's crazy ass is, and I know she's your friend."

I almost blew it by correcting him on that "friend" comment. Those bitches were *not* my friends. But I had to keep everybody thinking that they were until I got my revenge.

"Hey, before I get back to work, do you remember that letter I wrote you?" I wanted to give him a heads-up that this trip would not strictly be for gambling. I wanted to make sure he understood me before I wasted three days with him.

"It ran across my mind once your secretary invited me. I'm going to make up for turning you down back then. I'll see you in two weeks."

My plans were in motion, and my last prey was Tyrone. It would take more than a smile to convince him, though. Tyrone knew I had been hanging around with Keisha because she was using his car to meet up with me. If I was going to start working on Tyrone's ass, I needed to start now.

I took the rest of the day off since my senior accountants had everything under control, and I headed to my daddy's house.

Keisha told me she had to go to the Department of Human Services and recertify. She also said that would be an all-day process, and she would have his car. Not risking the chance of getting caught talking to Tyrone, I called her to see what she was doing just to know her location.

"Girl, I'm at this damn county building waiting to see my worker about my food stamps. This motherfucka is packed too. I missed my twelve o'clock appointment, but she said she would squeeze me in around three, so I'm just waiting on her with TJ's bad ass. Why? What's up?"

I still had a lot of work to do, so keeping things friendly became mandatory. "Soon as you leave there, call me so we can take TJ to Chuck E. Cheese. I got business to handle later, so call me soon as you see your worker." She agreed and gave me a second meeting with Tyrone today.

"Savannah, can you do me a favor? Can you take TJ to Tyrone after we leave Chuck E. Cheese, please? I met this cute-ass security guard, and we got plans to meet up about seven. I asked Tyrone to have his mama keep TJ because I know his sorry ass ain't gon' watch him. Savannah, I'm in love with a dog, girl."

She was referencing Tyrone when she said dog, but what was she considered? She was about to go fuck and suck a security guard she had just met. I'm not pointing fingers, but she ain't the one to talk like I'm not.

"Yes, I will drop him off. That will give me time to see my daddy." We ended the call, and I approached Tyrone's dope spot, which was on a crate behind the liquor store.

"Hey, Tyrone, have you seen Keisha?" I hadn't thought out a plan yet, but it was too late to withdraw my question.

"Naw, I ain't seen her ass. She said she had to do something about her food stamps and TJ was going too. I know I need my car."

I almost forgot she was in his car. She was going to go meet up with the security guard without even trying to bring Tyrone his car. What if he had to go somewhere? "Was there somewhere you needed to go? Or something you had to do?" What a perfect unplanned plan. I would chauffeur him as long as it wasn't drug-related.

"I ain't ate since nine this morning, and it's almost two. I'm hungry. Why? Are you volunteering to let me ride with you to get me something to eat?"

I walked closer to him so I wouldn't announce the next words to anyone that may have been listening. "As long as you leave your work behind, I'll take you wherever you need to go. I have two hours free."

Tyrone told me to meet him at his mama's house in ten minutes, and then walked down the alley. As I was walking back to my car, Javier was coming out of the store.

"What are you doing back there?"

I felt busted, but before I could answer, he kept talking.

"I've been texting you. Are you not getting my messages?"

That was a question I was prepared to answer. "No, I haven't had time to pay my cell phone bill. I'll do it tonight. Text me around eight."

I was using my Nextel phone because I had really forgotten to pay my T-Mobile bill, and that was the number I had given everybody at the park except for Keisha. I gave her my business line. I needed her to be able to contact me at all times.

"You got a T-Mobile, right?"

I answered, "Yes."

He confirmed my number, and then said, "I'm going to go pay it now. I can't wait until eight. I'm trying to see you at eight, if you know what I mean."

I knew exactly what he meant, and I agreed to the meeting because the last videotape I recorded of us fucking was so dark it was hard to recognize him except for his hair. I needed a clear shot, which meant I needed to keep the lights on. My bill was $340, so if he paid that in full, he deserved another ride.

Tyrone's mother was on the porch when I pulled up. She waved at my car, and then started screaming at Tyrone to come out. We had talked at the barbeque so there wasn't a need to go catch up with her now.

Tyrone jumped in my car. "Take me to M&Ms by the mall. I got a hunger for soul food." He handed me twenty dollars for gas. I told him I would give it to TJ tonight when I took him to Chuck E. Cheese.

"So, what's up with you and Keisha being all close and shit? I know y'all were buddies as kids, but she used to dog yo' ass, and now you came back balling with a good-ass job, and you treat her like she ain't done shit to you. You went to the South and got saved or something, huh?"

He was smarter than I thought. "No, silly, I didn't go get saved. We were kids then. Now if she pulls that shit on me as an adult, it will be handled differently than I handled it back then. I just believe in karma, and whatever she has done to me or anybody, she'll get it back."

I turned my head as I got on the 110 freeway. Tyrone laid his seat back some, and then continued talking.

"Well, I don't believe in karma. I believe in fate. She has done a lot of people dirty and has suffered no consequences for it. So, karma is not coming her way. I think she'll have to face fate on the shit she's done."

I urged him to elaborate, since he had me interested. "So, you think she may be killed or something?" I tried to sound concerned and not excited.

"It could be death; it could be AIDS. She could end up paralyzed from the waist down. What I'm saying is with karma, if you treat somebody bad, you will be treated badly back. You still have the chance to treat somebody good so you can be treated well. With fate, there isn't a chance given to fix fate. Once you are sentenced by fate, it's a life sentence. You feel me?"

It seems to me Tyrone had put some real thought into karma and fate. He must have had time while he was in jail.

"I like how you just broke that down to me. Guess you are more than a basketball player and drug dealer." I licked my lips and cut my eyes at him.

"Yeah, there's a lot I can do, and if you gave me a chance to show you, I'd make you a believer." He unlocked the door and started getting out. "Savannah, don't act like your country ass don't want nothing. Come in. I know it was all that corn bread you was eating down there that got your ass so fat."

I did want some greens and peach cobbler if they had some. I had lived in Georgia for the last ten years, and I missed the food. We sat in a booth in the back alone so we could continue our conversation, which he seemed eager to do.

"So, how did your man feel when you told him you were moving back to California? Don't start talking shit to me to me like you did Christina. I can tell by your hips and thighs you getting dick."

He took a bite into his smothered chicken. Something about Tyrone made me want to be real with him as much as I could without giving him insight on my plan of revenge.

"I wouldn't call him my man. We just did our thing time to time. To be real with you, he went to jail, so I didn't have to tell him shit. He lived with his baby mama. That was her responsibility."

Tyrone looked as if he saw a ghost. "Damn, no more good girl, I see." We both laughed a little.

"No more good girl. The way I see it, if I want to sample someone's goods, then I should be free to have them. I'm not the marriage type, nor do I want kids. No offense, but I'm not a Keisha, Christina, or Melinda. I don't fuck just because I can when I'm bored, or when I'm paid to. I do it when it's a need or if it becomes a desire. Do you understand me?" Looking at his face, I could see he understood completely.

"Keisha is my baby mama, that's all. I knew she was a ho before I fucked her. I didn't try to get her pregnant. TJ was an accident, but DNA said he was my accident. She had five niggas from the hood tested at the same time. All of them left with a smile on their faces but me. You don't have to apologize for calling her a ho. I do every day."

On the ride back, Keisha called me. I told Tyrone it was her calling, and he said, "Don't tell her we together." She was done and was ready to meet me at my daddy's house. I told her to go straight to Chuck E. Cheese, and I would meet her there. I dropped Tyrone off and headed straight to Bell. I would get to see him when I dropped TJ off tonight.

When I made it to Chuck E. Cheese, I wasn't surprised when she had the security guard in the car with her. "Girl, we decided to go out to eat in Pasadena and see a movie. You don't mind keeping him alone, do you? Just drop him off to his daddy when he's done. Oh, and he ran out of diapers too. I'll pay you back next time I see you. Thank you, Savannah."

Her flashlight cop was breaking his neck to check me out. What a loser. I told her I would take TJ to get diapers first, and then to a different Chuck E. Cheese. She pulled off without even saying bye to her child. She was a sorry-ass mother. I can point fingers on this one because I gave my child away when I knew I wasn't going to be a good mother.

She kept her child, yet put him off on everybody to get a steady income from the government while she continued living her life. That was wrong of her, and TJ would grow up hating her for it.

Keisha was helpful in more ways than one, however. I went to Sam's Club, bought a box of bulk diapers, and drove them to Tyrone, who was sitting outside on his mama's porch. He was so damned sexy.

"TJ, what are you doing, boy? You can't be bringing your pretty women around me, man." He grabbed the diapers and baby from me.

"We're headed to Chuck E. Cheese, but he didn't have any diapers, so I bought some and decided to drop them off over here before we left."

Tyrone was pissed. "That bitch always sending my son off to somebody with no diapers. He soaking wet. Come in while I change his clothes."

Ms. Maple's house looked the same. She still had everything wrapped in plastic. As a kid, I would get stuck to her couch or leave with a water stain on my back.

Ms. Maple and my daddy played spades together at least twice a week. I spent many hours with Tyrone, Memphis, and their friends. That's how my crush on Big Ant started, over at Ms. Maple's house. I don't care what time of day it was. She was always cooking something.

"I got a pot of greens on in there, Savannah. If you were missing some Southern cooking, you should have told me to fix you some. You know I'm from Louisiana. It will be ready around seven o'clock, so you come back, you hear? I'm going to make you some real peach cobbler too."

There was no turning her down, either. "Yes, ma'am, I'll be back with your grandson by then. I'm taking him to Chuck E. Cheese."

She smiled, and then took him from his daddy. "Take his daddy with you too. He needs to get away from here. All he does is walk the streets. Get him out of my face, please."

"Thank you, Ms. Maple. You heard your mama, Tyrone. Let's head out before it gets too late."

I honestly had a great time with Tyrone and TJ. Tyrone was a great father. Keisha didn't see that because she was too busy living her own life.

When I dropped them off, Tyrone ran in the house with TJ and came back with my plate of food and peach cobbler. It smelled so good. Once he handed me the plates, I heard the words I wanted to hear flow with ease out of Tyrone's mouth.

"Ay, Savannah, from our conversation earlier . . . If you ever need it, I got it for you."

I played dumb. "Need what, Tyrone?"

He looked over his shoulder, and then down the street. "If you ever need some dick, I got you covered."

How straightforward. No jive with it. "Tyrone, I don't think you can handle my needs." I turned my back to him and got back into my car, smiling ear to ear. He was a man with an ego . . . of course, attached to his dick.

"Give me a chance to prove it to you then."

I started my car and drove off.

Chapter 10

Ghostly Visions

The next few days that went by, I either gained a conscience or needed glasses. On my way to lunch with Stephanie, I could have sworn I saw Dre getting on the elevator as I was walking out. I did a double take, but the doors had closed before I could get a better look.

Then yesterday, as I ran along Venice Beach at 5:00 a.m., I thought I saw him sitting at one of the bus stops watching me. When I started walking that way, the bus pulled up and the look-alike got on. Sade's birthday was that weekend, so that's what I chalked up the visuals of Dre to.

I couldn't wait to go to Vegas with Big Ant. I was going to celebrate my daughter's birthday and get revenge at the same time.

I realized I only saw red since I was back in contact with Keisha and her crew. I had to get them back and prove to these hoes that the tables had turned, and *I* was the most desirable. I would avenge the way I was treated in the past, get to have sex with one of the men I was interested in back in the day, all the while celebrating my baby's birthday. If I won anything, it would get placed on her prepaid card to go along with her gift.

I knew I needed to check the PO Box next week because I was sure the Jeffersons would send pictures. They had sent a letter two months ago saying that they decided to tell Sade they were not her parents, but her godparents. They wanted her to know she had a mother and father out there who loved her and still took care of her, but they were just too far away to see her.

I woke up at 5:00 a.m. Friday morning to get prepared for my trip with Big Ant. I needed to pick him up without being seen, so I asked him to meet me behind our old elementary school, which was in walking distance from his house. As an extra precaution, I drove my Chrysler, which I hadn't driven to my old neighborhood so no one knew I owned one. It had been painted too. It was now burnt orange and trimmed in silver with cream interior.

I had packed two Louis Vuitton travel bags, not knowing what I wanted to wear. Usually when I'm in Las Vegas, I go to the outlets for a little shopping, but I wanted to party this trip.

The crush I had on Ant was still there, and he had gotten even more handsome. They didn't call him Big Ant as a cliché like they called fat guys Slim. He had earned his nickname. Big Ant was seven foot one and weighed about 250 pounds. Everything on him was huge—or at least I hoped so.

When we were younger, he would grip basketballs in each of his huge hands and pretend to throw them at us without ever letting one go. He was a lot of man, even back then. He was a gorgeous big man. He had tight, slanted eyes like mine, but he really had Asian heritage. He was born from an Army brat of the Vietnam War. His mother was half Vietnamese and black.

He wasn't bright-skinned, yet he was far from being dark; more like a toffee color. He had his daddy's big lips and ears that sat to the side of his face like minisatellites, but they didn't affect him being handsome.

This may sound weird, but Ant always had this fresh laundry scent, which made me want to smell him. I would push past people to sit next to him just to inhale his fragrance.

When I made it to the school, he was sitting on the steps that lead to the gym. "Man, sitting up here brought back all kinds of memories. I remember the first day I sat and watched you really hoop. Savannah, you had a shot."

I smiled and thanked him. "Ant, we have four hours on this road. Can you roll up so we can stop in about an hour and eat?" He dug in his bag and pulled out two tamales.

"I already thought about that. You know she came by screaming so I copped us one."

I wasn't trying to be mean, but my mouth was my worst enemy. "I wouldn't dare eat another bathtub tamale. It can't be safe. You enjoy tasting Marie and Poncho's dirty asses, and in an hour, I'll stop and get me something to eat."

There was a look of disappointment on his face. "All right, I'll taste Marie's ass, but don't act like you haven't tasted her ass before. You used to get paper food stamps from your daddy and buy like eight of them with your fat ass. I see a lot has changed. Your ass is still fat, but now when I say that, I mean your butt and not your body."

I was two seconds away from snapping on his ass about bringing up me and food stamps or me being overweight as a child, and then he pointed out my changes—smart man.

We smoked and talked for two hours before my hunger caught up with me, so we pulled over

in Barstow and ate at IHOP. Ant held the door
open for me as I walked in. Once he was fully in,
three little boys ran up to him and asked for his
autograph.

I laughed because I assumed the kids thought
he was an NBA superstar because of his height,
weight, and the way he was wearing dark glasses
until one of the little boys said, "Mr. Wallace, is
it true you're going to a NBA training camp this
year?"

Ant shook the little boy's head with his hand
and said, "Yes, it's true. I can't play college
basketball forever, can I, man?"

The little boy said, "No," and his father
approached and shook Ant's hand.

"You gave them hell last month, son." Ant
looked the older white man directly in his face,
giving him full eye contact, and thanked him.

We made it to our table with the entire restaurant watching us. "What was all that about?"

Come to find out, Mr. Anthony Wallace was
a big-time college basketball star at California
State University at Berkley. My uncle had said
Keisha's sister, who I still hadn't managed to
see or find out who she was, and I were the
only two who made it. He must have meant out
of the girls, because everyone seemed to know
Anthony Wallace, power forward from Cali.

"What the hell are you still doing walking around South Central LA like a nobody? I can't believe you even sleep down there when you're in town. You don't have to put up with them lowlifes."

He put his index finger over my mouth. "Damn, you talk too much, and you always talking shit. My mama and daughter live there, and that's where I'm from. Even if I get picked up by a NBA team, I'm doing my mama just like you did your daddy. I'm going to hook her house up, get her a security gate and a nice-ass alarm system. I'm going to keep a little change in my boys' pockets like Tyrone and Javier, who ain't never leaving the hood, to keep her extra protected. Now shut up and order you something so we can get ready to party."

He was dumb as fuck to think his life would be that easy as a celebrity, but who am I to bust his bubble? He would learn the hard way.

Once we arrived at the hotel, we showered separately and hit the casino. We started at the crap tables, and then ended up playing blackjack. It was too hot in the daytime to move around, so we decided to gamble at the same hotel we were staying at until sunset.

Ant was more of a gentleman than I thought. Every chair I sat in, he pulled out, doors I went through, he ran to open, and he paid for every drink I ordered that didn't come free.

He suggested we put on our party clothes now so we would not have to go back to the room anytime soon. I didn't want to be the party pooper, but I was really enjoying myself with him and didn't want to be separated by the loud environment of the club, so I asked to go sightseeing instead.

I arranged a two-hour-long limousine ride around the Strip with stops made at our request. I had never had so much fun. Ant made the driver stop where Tupac was shot and made him block traffic on an already busy street while we paid our respects. Ant said a few words of thanks to the deceased rapper with his lighter lit.

I had passed this area at least eight or nine times, and it never crossed my mind that one of my favorite rappers was shot below my wheels. I hate that "out of sight, out of mind" shit, and I do it all the time. I was crying my eyes out at my high school's football game when the radio DJ announced he died in the hospital. I played all his songs on repeat and promised to stay a devoted fan. Almost fifteen years later, I had to be reminded by a man five years younger than myself to never forget his legacy.

We rapped every Tupac song that we could think of. Later, Ant said he had done the same for Biggie in Hollywood. He loved both rappers in different ways and couldn't place one over the other. He thanked them both for paving the way.

After we were done rapping our heads off, he asked me to close my eyes. "How can you ask me to close my eyes? I can't stop smiling and laughing long enough to see out of them now."

Throwing his hands up, he said, "Just shut up for once. Damn, your mouth will make you miss out on a lot of shit." I rolled my eyes, and then closed them.

He kissed my lips softly four times, and then went into my mouth with his tongue and wrapped it around mine. I felt him dig in his pocket. I could tell he didn't want the kiss to end, but he needed to find whatever he was looking for in his pocket.

Ant pulled out a hundred-dollar bill and handed it to the driver. He had won $1,500 on the crap table. "Ay, man, give us one more hour and roll up that window." He pointed to the tinted window that separated us from the driver, and then continued kissing my lips.

In between those kisses, he managed to say, "Sorry I turned you down when we were kids. I know I fucked up. Lie back so I can make it up to you."

I was down for some freaky shit, but fucking in the backseat of a limo with a driver was a little bit much. "Ant, you must be drunk. I am not fucking you in the back of this limo, and you need to start thinking like a future celebrity. What if he sells this to a tabloid? I could just see it now—NBA superstar fucks childhood friend in the backseat of a limo while holding a memorial for Tupac and Biggie."

He covered my mouth with his hand and cut me off. "Na-Na, whatever happens in Vegas stays in Vegas. Ain't that why you brought me here?"

He continued kissing me, but not before I was able to get out, "Don't call me Na-Na."

After laying me back on the seat, he ate the hell out of my pussy. I watched his ears flap like Dumbo flying away . . . That's how fast he was moving his head. It felt so good. The only thing killing the mood was that I kept getting stuck to the leather seat.

I could see the driver watching us more than the road. Something about the driver watching turned me on even more, so I pulled my titties out so he could have something nice to look at. I lay back and let Ant eat my pussy all the way back to the hotel. He didn't even attempt to fuck me. When the limo stopped, he licked his lips and drank the champagne straight from the bottle.

It was now a quarter to 10:00 p.m., and even though I had done a lot of drinking, the head he gave me made me hungry.

"Can we please go eat now?"

Ant flagged down a cab. "What type of food you want to eat? 'Cause all I'm trying to eat tonight is you."

He hadn't even washed his face. "You are not riding around Las Vegas with my pussy all over your face."

He jumped in the cab, then said, "Watch me!"

I shook my head and said, "Seafood."

The cabdriver took us to this nice little crab shack that also served lobsters. The food was great. After we had eaten, we called it a night to rest for Saturday night. I thought Ant would be mad when he saw me headed to the other bedroom and not the one he was already occupying. Instead, he yelled, "I'll get your ass tomorrow."

I couldn't believe it, but I didn't wake up until almost two in the afternoon Saturday. When I came out of the bedroom of our two-bedroom suite, Ant was on the floor working out.

"You know there *is* a gym here, right?"

He stopped his crunches. "I was there all morning, sleepyhead. Go back to sleep if you going to start talking shit. As a matter fact, I'm ordering us some room service. You can't talk with your mouth full."

He thought he was so funny, so I ate in silence. I didn't say anything to him for two hours. It was almost five when I opened my mouth.

"It's our last day here, and I want to enjoy it. Can we start drinking now and have a late dinner if we get hungry?" I tried hard to sound ticked off.

Ant walked over to the refrigerator and pulled out another bottle of champagne. "Let's do it, baby." We killed that bottle and ordered two more that had the same fate as the first. I was sloppy drunk and more horny than drunk.

"So, is that how you do, Ant? Eat a woman's pussy, then leave her fiending for the dick?" He stood over me.

"I showed you what my mouth was about. How about giving me a sample of yours?"

I wasn't totally out of it, but I remembered that I had set up the video camera in my room in the closet and had it set on zoom facing the bed when we first arrived.

"I'm going to suck your dick in here right now, but when we done, I want to you to take me in my bedroom and you fuck the shit out of me doggie style. Can you handle that?"

He chuckled. "Yeah, I can handle that. Get your drunken ass in the bed now. This liquor got me, and I need to pee. When I get in there, have that ass in the air."

My plan seemed to work like clockwork. I went and hit record, and before he made it to the room, I was at the head of the bed with my ass in the air, waiting on him to come and pound me.

He rested his dick on my back while he opened the condom. At first, I thought it was his hand because it was heavy, but just as I thought . . . Everything on his body was big.

When he slid his dick inside of me, he cupped both of my breasts in his hands and started pounding me. There weren't any feelings behind it, either. When I started telling him he was in too deep, he went deeper.

"Shut yo' ass up and take this dick. This how you wanted it, didn't you?"

I screamed out, "Yes!"

Ant let my breasts go and gripped a handful of my hair dead in the center of my head and forced me to look in his direction.

He kissed me while he stroked, which made his dick slide into a less painful position. "Bite my lip, Savannah."

I sucked his bottom lip until the majority was in my mouth and bit down on it.

He pulled his lip away and pushed my face into the pillow and held his hand over my head so I couldn't lift it up and went deeply all over again.

I felt the come slide down my legs. "Damn, this pussy good, girl. I knew it was going to be." Ant tucked his arms under my armpits until his arms wrapped over my shoulders and laid me down backward on his dick.

I screamed out, "Ant!" because his dick felt like it was piercing my guts.

"You on top now, baby. Show me how much dick you want in you."

I went down on the dick to the halfway point, came back up, and then went down on it again.

"Savannah, you can take more dick than that." He moved me off him and flipped me over. This big nigga moved fast. He placed my legs in the air and, with one hand, held both of my feet together and started fucking me slightly sideways. I came again. "I can't wait 'til you're my girl so I can take this condom off. That pussy getting wet as hell. I know it's some killer."

He closed his eyes and turned his head up to the ceiling. The grand finale was just seconds away, and I wanted to egg him on. I started moaning louder until it was in full words.

"Fuck me, Ant, fuck me. Fuck me, make me come, daddy, Ant, fuck me!" It was working like a charm.

He put his head back down and started looking at me in my eyes. I licked my lips, bit my bottom one, and heard the words I had wanted to hear. "Oh, shit, Savannah, I'm about to nut," and his river came flowing.

It was hard as hell to get myself dressed to impress after getting some good dick like that, and I was still drunk. I did my best, though. I put on an all-white, tie-around-the-neck dress that stopped three inches under my butt. I put the stilettos I brought to wear with the dress back in the box and put on my backup all-white pumps. I went over the layers in my hair with my flatiron, applied a little lipstick, and was ready to go.

There must have been a memo sent out, because Ant walked out of the room in all white too, and boy, was he looking good. I ran back in the room and used a feminine wipe to absorb the new wetness looking at him brought on. That nigga could dress.

When I came out of the room, he was posing for me. "You can say it, baby, a nigga look good, don't I?"

Not wanting to pump his head up, I replied, "You straight, slightly above average."

He took my hand and said, "That's cool. You can hate. Your pussy already told me what was up." Then we headed for a night on the town.

We fell into some club in a new casino on the Strip. It was packed and jumping. The bouncer recognized who he was at the door, let us in free, and then led us to the VIP section. The place was filled with celebrities.

Surprisingly, he didn't seem excited when he saw who our company was. Instead, he acted the same way everyone else did.

I didn't want to be under him the whole night so after an hour or so, I went to mingle with the non-VIP clubgoers. I danced with about five different men before making my way to the bar. When I looked at the VIP section, Ant was covered with women. I didn't want to look like a hater, so I got comfortable.

"What is a pretty thing like you doing sitting at the bar and not dancing with me?"

The voice was deep, like Barry White's, and him whispering in my ear sent chills down my spine. Standing in front of me was this heap of black beauty. His aura was of a Greek god or African war hero. If it wasn't for the flashing lights and his cream-colored suit, I wouldn't have been able to see him. Brother was black. He smelled of cocoa butter and Blue Magic hair grease. I couldn't make out his features completely, but he was fine enough to dance with. We danced for three songs straight, which all seemed to be neo-soul songs.

After the dance, he took me back to where he found me at the bar, took a seat next to me, and bought us both a drink. We talked about our careers and life for almost an hour before Ant came and asked me to dance with him.

"Are you enjoying yourself, Savannah?"

With my head on his chest, I nodded my head yes.

"I was watching you dance with Color Purple over there, and that's when I realized I came here with the prettiest woman in Nevada tonight." A flower man came by and offered me a flower for Ant to buy. I turned down the offer.

"No, ma'am, the guy at the bar just bought it for you." I turned to face the bar, but there was no one there. Ant, the flower man, and I searched through the club trying to see who bought it for me. Finally, the flower man pointed to the door, and there was a man leaving with dreads. Was that Dre?

Suddenly, I snapped at the flower man. "What did he look like? Did he have a tattoo on his face? Huh? Answer me! Did he have a Southern accent? Could you make out his eye color?"

The flower man seemed scared. "I couldn't see his face, ma'am, and he didn't sound like he had an accent."

Ant stood in front of me. "What's wrong, Savannah? Are you okay? Who do you think that was?"

I wasn't sure who that was or if it was Dre. After five drinks at the club and the champagne at the hotel, there was nothing I could say to Ant except, "You want to smoke?"

And then I headed out of the club to go vomit on Las Vegas's beautiful Strip. Happy third birthday, Sade.

Chapter 11

The New Intern

After all the visions of Dre, I decided to speed up my acts of revenge. The weekend after my trip to Las Vegas with Big Ant was when Tyrone showed me he was the weakest link in his crew. It had been almost two weeks since that disappointing sexual encounter.

I was back to work and focused. I had fucked all the "Hoes Crew's" men—or should I say, babies' daddies—and would let stage two of my plans hold off until I found out if my company was really going to open an office in Seattle, Washington. If they did, I would be moving there, which would be closer to Sade and far away from the drama I was about to cause in California.

When I made it to work, Stephanie told me there was a certified letter waiting for me on my desk. Whenever I heard *letter*, I automatically thought it had something to do with Dre. This time it didn't.

The letter was from Dr. Davis reminding me to have my ovarian cysts looked at and informing me of her moving her practice to Memphis, Tennessee. I hadn't thought about those little circles they found on my ultrasound since the doctor brought it to my attention. She said that cysts were common in African American women and didn't really push the issue for me to have them checked out, so I didn't. I will also put that on my things-to-do list, right next to Will's handsome ass.

Ever since Tyrone called himself talking shit to me after his three minutes of nothing, I've wanted to fuck his best friend. That would be the cherry on top of my ice cream of revenge.

I didn't have time to set up any appointments right now, not to see my doctor in Memphis, Tennessee, or Will. I had two interns who had started almost two weeks ago that I had never met. I decided to be the best boss of the year and treat them both to a two-hour lunch in Hollywood at Universal CityWalk's Hard Rock Café.

When I arrived, they were already seated at a table enjoying the live band. When I introduced myself, they both stood and the relaxed look they had on their faces while I was walking to the table seemed to evaporate. They were businesspeople. I loved it.

"There are two things I don't play about and those are my business and my past. Since this lunch has nothing to do with either, you both can relax. I want to get to know you and your personalities."

Neither one of them sat down until I took my seat. I felt like a judge. "Well, let's start this off with a round of drinks. I want to congratulate you both on making it this far in college. Of course, after our lunch, I will be sending you home with full credit for today. I can't have you feeling like happy hour on the job."

There was something about Erika that looked familiar. I didn't want to keep looking her way, but I really wanted to know where I had known her from. It wasn't a negative feeling when I looked at her, but I couldn't place a positive one there, either. She was too young to have played basketball with or against me as a teenager. Maybe it was her college look that made me feel like I knew her. I don't know, but I didn't want to make her uncomfortable while I tried to find out.

Once we ate and said good-bye, I headed back to the office to start working on the new contract for our Seattle location.

The opening of a location in Washington and not Chicago was my idea, so I headed this deal. We had grossed Strax Industries more money than previously estimated. As a show of appreciation, not only did we receive bonuses, but they brought in new business. We decided to dedicate the majority of the Los Angeles location to them and work other accounts at a new facility.

"Stephanie, when you're done, I need you for a second." Stephanie had become my personal partner. She had even decided to make the move to Washington with me.

She said, "What would you do in Washington without me, Savannah? Count me in."

I would go crazy without her, and she knew it. "Yes, Savannah, what's up?" All this California sunshine was doing Stephanie some good. She had started dating a Los Angeles firefighter, and I could tell he was fucking the shit out of her. She even had a new walk.

"I have some updates I need you to make in my planner, please." Stephanie closed the door and sat on the table. "Did you fuck Tyrone yet?" She was smiling ear to ear.

When I told Stephanie my plan of revenge, she said, "This is some real-life *Kill Bill* shit." She kept tally of everything I did, everybody I fucked, and who I was getting payback on in my planner. When I asked her why she felt the need to keep up with it, she replied, "Beatrix Kiddo kept a list." That girl watched too many movies.

"Yes, I fucked his sorry ass for three whole minutes, and then the bastard went to sleep on me."

She fell out laughing. I mean, tears formed in Stephanie's eyes. This shit was so funny to her.

"This shit ain't funny, girl."

She tried to stop laughing. "At least you got fucked good by Big Ant, the future NBA star. He had your side hurting for days after he beat you down."

Big Ant had put a beating on me. My side killed me for days. As a matter of fact, it was still hurting, but BC Powder helped ease the pain. I had dicks his size before, but never did they cause as much damage as his dick. He needs a warning label on his drawers.

"So, when can I have some pussy, or do I need to drive around putting out fires first?"

She smiled, "Anytime you want some pussy, you know where you can get it."

It wasn't that I really wanted to fuck Stephanie. I just wanted to make sure I still could. We had been in California going on three years, and I had only fucked her twice. She met her fireman six months after we arrived and had been fucking him since. It couldn't have been too serious because he was married and could only see her once every other month, but like I predicted, her first piece of dick she would get attached to. I bet he couldn't even fuck. If Stephanie and I weren't so close, I would fuck his fine ass to see.

"Can you arrange a dinner with me and Will from the sheriff's office for his first available date? I put his number in that planner you protect so dearly."

She went flipping through the pages. "So, you have already contacted him? Look at you being the aggressor."

She would never believe it if I told her the truth, so I didn't bother. The truth was that I pretended to have jury duty and was the lost jurywoman who couldn't find her courtroom. I was directed to the sheriff's office for more assistance and passed him on my way there. There was some small talk, and I threw in a "We should do lunch and catch up," and he had agreed. He had plans to hoop with Tyrone that evening and invited me to watch, but I hadn't fucked Tyrone yet, so I didn't want to screw up my plans.

"Don't answer me then, Savannah. I'll set it up and let you know the time and place." I had a conference call to update Williams and Williamson on the upcoming venture in Washington, and then headed home. Thank God it was Thursday. Just one more day of the workweek.

Since I handled all my company's business Thursday, I took Friday off to chill with Keisha. I wanted her to feel the exact same way I felt when she fucked Kevin. I really thought she was my friend back then, and she needed to think I was her friend now.

"Wake your ass up, Keisha, I'm on my way."

There was some hesitation in her voice. "Tyrone, umm. Tyrone spent the night with us last night, and he hasn't left yet."

She sounded as if I interrupted her boring-ass sex with him. "Tell Tyrone I said hi, and all he got is three minutes to finish up the job because I'm on my way and he better not fall asleep."

I hung up the phone before she heard my laughter. I laughed so hard both of my sides began throbbing. It felt like I was period bloated, yet there was pain with it. This was the worst the pain had gotten. I had to lie across my bed for a minute until the pain subsided. I swallowed two extra-strength Tylenol and headed out the door.

When I pulled up to Keisha's house, Tyrone was getting in his car to leave. I decided to talk shit to him.

"Why are you leaving so quickly, speedy? Do you ever slow down or do you just like finishing fast? I know you got three minutes for me like usual, don't you, Tyrone? What's wrong? My cat got your tongue? No, that couldn't be right because your tongue was just as sorry as your dick. I should go in here and tell Keisha about the sorry-ass performance you gave me, but that would break her heart, wouldn't it? The love of her life, Tyrone, fucked her new best friend from her past."

He closed his car door, walked up to me, and grabbed me by my neck, shaking me. "Bitch, if you ever tell her about us, I will beat your ass myself, do you hear me? You a ho anyways. You better hope Christina don't find out you fucked Javier and about him paying your cell phone bill or she might just introduce you to her box cutter. I don't know what you trying to pull by fucking your homegirls' baby daddies, but you barking up the wrong tree. You're going to get what you asking for, Savannah. Keep playing with people's lives and you're going to lose yours." He let me go and spit on my windshield. "Fuck your karma, Savannah. Prepare for your fate." He pushed me out of his way, told me to get my car out of the fucking way, and then drove off.

He was so caught up with fate that he didn't realize that karma helped determined your fate. I was giving those hoes back what they gave me. He was wrong to say karma and fate didn't work together. Karma was the beginning, and fate was the ending.

Why in the fuck did Javier tell Tyrone about us, anyway? I could kill Javier for telling him. I wanted all six of them to know, but not until I had finished my exit plan from California. I had at least four months left here, and I didn't want to have to deal with drama in them.

When I made it to the door, I made Keisha call Christina and Melinda and invite them with us. I picked them up, and we headed to the spa. During our massages, I got an earful of girl talk. It was like a movie script.

Christina: "Did you find out who Ant went to Vegas with yet, girl?"

Melinda: "Naw, he sticking to his story. He supposedly went with an ex-teammate from high school. I don't believe his lying ass."

Keisha: "I told you not to worry about that shit. I'll get it out of Tyrone. You know y'all's baby daddies tell him everything. Soon as I find out, you know I'm going to tell you. Savannah, aren't you glad you ain't got to go through this stupid shit with niggas?"

I stayed silent and hummed an, "uh-huh," just to give some kind of response.

Melinda: "Well, if I find out it was with a bitch, I'm going back to jail. Y'all remember what happened the last time he called himself fucking another bitch."

Christina: "Yeah, I do, I'm still on probation for the shit, bitch."

Keisha: "We did beat her ass kind of bad. That bitch had blood everywhere."

There was a roar of laughter. When did these bitches get bite behind their bark? I remember when they had a no-fight rule because they refused to mess up their faces. Was Tyrone's threat about Christina and a box cutter valid? I tried not to think about it, but the longer I stayed around all three of them, the more I found out that these bitches were crazy.

Keisha had been arrested while pregnant with TJ for hitting a girl over her head with a chair at the food stamp office because she found out Tyrone had gotten some head from her. What had I set myself up for? "I thought y'all said that y'all weren't with your baby daddies anymore." It flew out of my mouth. I hoped they couldn't detect the nervousness in my tone.

Christina was more than happy to answer. "We not, but they will *always* be our men. They report to us like we report to them. Javier has started shit with every nigga I have tried to fuck with after breaking up with him."

Melinda finished it up for her. "Ant and Tyrone have too. We can't be with each other, but we be damned before we sit back and allow each other to fuck with somebody else too."

Smiling, I said, "Y'all crazy for that one." All the while, I was thinking I needed to destroy the tapes and as a precaution, I would stay away from them until I was out of California. My plan of getting revenge was over. I had to live with the satisfaction of knowing I got my payback without sharing it with them. If they ever found out, they wouldn't be devastated—they would join up and whip my ass, and then sit around the jailhouse laughing about it.

I wasn't prepared to fight anybody. That's why I had bought a gun, which did me no good because I left it in my nightstand for safety. Maybe it was time to start carrying it around.

It was 10:00 p.m. when I dropped them all off at Keisha's house. Tyrone, Javier, Ant, and a few other dudes were sitting on their cars rapping when we pulled up.

"Ay, Savannah, I got a boy in Nevada who got the hookup on T-Mobile phones. You want his number? He said he can even get your bill paid for a small fee." Tyrone must have found out about Ant and me too, because Ant turned his head when Tyrone was done.

Niggas talked like bitches. When was it ever cool to be a bitch nigga? Was it the new style or fad? Men were supposed to act like men and leave the gossiping to the women. I was not going to sit here and let them make me feel like a ho. I fucked them, whether they saw it that way or not.

"Is this the same nigga we were talking about earlier? The real fast guy? If it is, tell him I'm good. I know somebody who fucked him and his whole crew. Made them feel like bitches, then sent them away. Plus, I heard him and his boys were bisexual. I heard they sit around like bitches talking about whom they fucked and what bills they paid to fuck. You should be careful of who you pick to be cool with."

Keisha had no idea what we were talking about, but she joined in. "I hate when niggas brag on their dicks. You right about that, Savannah. That is some bitch shit. I couldn't see a group of niggas huddled up giving each other pointers like women do. That just sounds gay."

That was all the confirmation I needed to leave my past alone. I felt like I had won a little bit when it came to the word war with Tyrone, but I needed to win when it came to getting revenge too. This time, it wasn't going to be over until I wanted it to be. I would sleep on it over the weekend and come up with a new plan. There was no way I was going to let my newfound fear of the "Hoes Crew" stop me, nor was the gossiping little bitches that called themselves niggas going to get away with it.

I called Stephanie to get an update on Will. "He said he wouldn't be free for a while, but he would call you at the office when he became available. Sorry, Savannah."

I told her good night and hung up the phone. When I pulled into my driveway, I got a call from Javier.

"Damn, Savannah, if you wanted to fuck me and my boys, why didn't you just tell me? We could have set up a group activity."

Speechless, I hung up the phone. I had gone from being the laughingstock of the girls as a teenager to the new ho joke between the men. I was so pissed off I didn't even get out of my car. I sat there going over every possible evil thought I could muster, and then I thought about Hollywood Boulevard—not for partying purposes, but prostitution. The one thing all seven of us had in common was we all liked sex with different people we hadn't had sex with before.

It was time to meet some new friends, preferably the scandalous type, which would do whatever I wanted them to do as long as I paid them.

I sent a text to Tyrone, Ant, and Javier asking them if they were down for a wild night with me and my real friends. I apologized to each of them and explained Georgia had turned me into a little freak, and I had some of my freaky friends from college coming in town who I'd love for them to meet.

I told them that I had honestly thought about fucking all three of them together, at the same time, and then decided against it and planned my individual time with them. I asked if they could keep my freaky ways from their babies' mamas and come live a day in my life Saturday night. They each agreed, even Tyrone, who tried to explain those pathetic three minutes he gave me was an accident. I told them all to meet me at my time-share property tomorrow at 8:00 p.m.

I had to move fast. It was already 11:00 p.m. Friday night, and I had a lot of planning to do. I knew I would need Stephanie in on this one, but I couldn't give her all the details or she would back out. I told her just enough to get her to agree.

This was going to be the craziest and deadliest shit I had ever done, but it was worth a try, and if I had my way, I would get all six of them at once. I drove down Sunset Boulevard and rounded up four of the nastiest-looking women I could find walking the street with pussy for sale and offered them each $1,000 to be active participants in my plan. All four agreed and said they would have done it for less.

I dropped them off at my rental property and told them they wouldn't be paid until the deed was done and I would be back in the morning to take them to the salon and shopping. My plan was to turn these pennies into silver dollars, even if it was for one night. I needed them to look their best, and I would pay whatever price to get it done.

When I arrived in the morning, I handed them all douches, soap, washrags, deodorant, sweats, and T-shirts. I didn't expect this to get the scent of the streets out of them, but to calm it down enough to take them shopping in the mall. When we got to the salon, I got three of them sew-in weaves and the other a short haircut like the one I used to wear.

By 5:00 p.m. that Saturday afternoon, I had a house full of Halle Berrys. You would have never known these women were walking the streets giving five-dollar blowjobs less than twenty-four hours ago.

Stephanie had been told my plan, and we set up two video cameras that would record the entire night, including the payment I had promised the women. I took before and after pictures too just in case the men didn't believe the women they screwed were full-time street-walkers.

This had turned out to be a $7,000 plan, and I hoped I got my money's worth. It took $250 just to get the scent of uncleanness off the women and out of the house.

I dimmed the lights and burned oils I had bought from the beach. The picture window that gave the prettiest view of the ocean I had ever seen was wide open to help with lighting.

The women had been told the plan, and I offered each an additional $500 if they could get the men to fuck them without a condom. There was nothing left to do but wait on the men to arrive.

While waiting, we all had a drink, and I gave the women their own blunt to smoke while Stephanie and I puffed on ours. Soon, one drink turned into two more drinks, and we were on our second blunt. I would die if these niggas stood me up tonight.

Chapter 12

Behind the Mask

It was ten minutes to 10:00 p.m. when the doorbell rang. Tyrone walked in first, leading the pack. "Well? What took y'all so long? We've been waiting." They were high as hell. Javier decided to be the spokesman of the group.

"Savannah, it was hard as hell getting away from your homegirls, and then we had to get some weed to bring out here. We drove the speed limit all the way here."

I wasn't mad at all. I was happy they finally came. I made introductions and offered them a seat. Tyrone asked for something to roll up on, so I handed him the yellow pages and turned on some music. Ant walked straight to the window to look at the view of the ocean.

"This is a nice-ass spot you got here, Savannah. You doing real good for yourself, I see." I reminded Ant he would have the same as soon as he signed that NBA contract. That is, if his baby mama didn't kill him for raw dogging prostitutes first.

Once the blunts were in rotation, the conversations started between the men and my new employees. Surprisingly, these women were smart. They were up to date on the sports and could hold an intelligent conversation. Their grammar was perfect and none of them used any street slang. They were making me proud.

Stephanie and I didn't join in on the weed smoking because we knew who our houseguests were behind their costumes. I've seen all the commercials that said you couldn't catch most STDs by kissing and so on, but I didn't believe the hype. If you can get strep throat during kissing, then you can catch anything from it in my opinion. I'm not saying the women had anything serious, but even an untreated yeast infection could be dangerous.

I made mixed drinks from cranberry juice and vodka and dropped two ecstasy pills in the blender with it. I used the X as an insurance policy to ensure everybody except me and Stephanie would be fucking tonight. Once the pills had dissolved, I added crushed ice to nine glasses, but only poured my version of the date rape drink into three of them.

I gave myself and all the ladies vodka and cranberry juice straight from the bottle. The blended drink was for the men only. The hoes didn't need help getting in the mood to fuck. It was their full-time job.

I waited thirty minutes for the drinks to kick in, and then it was time for me to get the party started. My idea was to treat Stephanie like my slut. If the niggas saw me getting some pussy, I was sure their egos would make them want some too. "Stephanie, come here, baby. Why are you way over there?"

Stephanie came and sat next to me. I pulled her in closer to me and kissed her. For added effect, I stuck my tongue out so they could see her suck on it.

Javier took the bait. "Damn, Savannah, it's like that?"

I stopped the kiss and rubbed on her fat-ass booty. "Yeah, it's like. Y'all got four beautiful women over there that want to see what Cali dick is like. Y'all got them covered, I hope. Or are y'all just going to watch me get some pussy?"

Javier turned his head and looked in the ladies' direction. I wasn't going to allow him to choose which one he wanted because he was Christina's baby daddy. I had already chosen his, Christina's, Tyrone's, and Keisha's fate.

"Amber and April, why don't you show my boys, Tyrone and Javier, some love. Ant, since you're the NBA superstar in here, you get star treatment. Denise and Brittney, show my boo a nice time."

I hoped Denise and Brittney didn't carry an incurable disease because Ant had a future. They looked the cleanest when we met them, but if they weren't, oh well, like Tyrone would say . . . It was his fate. The ladies moved closer to the men and did some pants rubbing, but I needed to speed things up. I went in the kitchen and poured another round of drinks for the men.

I made sure the glasses were filled to the top and rolled them up a blunt. I handed them their drinks. "Ay, fellows, don't you think them drinks would be better if y'all had some head to go with them? I'm just saying. The ladies aren't drinking or smoking. I think they should be doing something with their mouths, right? I hate to sound vulgar, but y'all hoes need to get to work." Tyrone dropped his pants first while killing his glass of drink.

"Hell, yeah, Savannah, they need to be using they mouth. I want some of that Southern hospitality. Can you make me another drink and turn on the air? It's getting hot in here." I made them another X on the rocks and watched the ladies suck them down.

Denise and Brittney stood Ant up against the wall and one was sucking his dick, the other was sucking and licking his balls, and then they switched. He was in ecstasy while on Ecstasy, and no one knew it but me. This was the part that I hid from Stephanie. I knew she wouldn't take part if she knew I planned to drug the men to get the job done.

Watching the men get head had really turned me on, so I pulled Stephanie's titties out of her dress and started sucking on them. All of the men watched as I did it. I laid her back on the couch, looked at them individually, and asked, "Y'all got condoms?"

Tyrone turned to Ant. "Nigga, that's what we were stopping at the store for. Damn, we were so high we forgot."

I jumped up and said, "I got some spermicide, that's all y'all really need it for. Two of my girls are almost doctors, the other is a nurse, and Denise is a biology major. What better women could you ask to go raw in?"

Ant seemed unsure, but before he could turn down my offer, the leader of the pack spoke up.

"That's cool. I'm just worried about another TJ. Go get it, Na-Na. I don't feel like driving to the store."

I wanted so badly to correct him. Instead, I walked into my bedroom and grabbed the spermicide. I emptied the whole bottle, rinsed it out, and filled it with 80 percent water and 20 percent baby oil. *Bet he'll wish he called me Savannah now.* I shook the bottle so the water would feel nice and slippery when they applied it.

When I joined the party, Javier was already bareback fucking Amber over my ottoman. Stephanie's ass must have been fucked up. When I walked in, she was naked, legs wide open, and Tyrone was playing with her pussy with his fingers.

"I got her, Tyrone, this wifey right here, you feel me?" I said, while handing him the bottle.

"Cool. April, why don't you get off your knees and show me how you ride this dick, baby? Man, Savannah, we owe you big time for this here. You like one of my niggas now." If he only knew what I had set him up for, he wouldn't be thanking me.

I took Stephanie by the hand and led her in the room. I had already told her we weren't fucking tonight. We would watch them in the other room fuck live on my television.

Tyrone nutted quickly again, but the X provided backup, and his dick grew back hard. I thought watching live porn in my house would turn me on, but instead, I felt disgusted. Tyrone was eating April's pussy like he knew her. I couldn't give him the benefit of the doubt and blame it on all the drugs because he went down on me easily too.

As a matter of fact, they all had eaten my pussy without me asking or hinting that I wanted it done. I continued watching, horrified.

Ant was killing Denise and Brittney. He had them on their knees on the floor, fucking them at the same time. He fucked Denise for three whole minutes, and then slid his dick in Brittney. The women were in pain with each stroke. You could tell by their faces that he was giving them the same dick he had given me in Vegas.

I set the alarm to go off in three hours, locked the bedroom door, and called it a night. The ladies had them covered, and in three hours, I would be kicking them out.

When the alarm sounded, everybody was asleep except Ant and Amber. He was on top of her in a lovemaking position with her titties in his mouth. When I walked in, Amber looked spooked.

"When you went to bed, each one of them fucked all of us. You were asleep so we couldn't ask."

Stupid, greedy-ass niggas. I gave each of them their own bitch to fuck, and they weren't satisfied. They had to get in four different pussies.

"Don't worry about it, Amber. Enjoy the dick, and when y'all done, come get me so we can get these men home before their baby mamas send a search party."

I went and replayed the footage to see what happened. It looked like the switch was caused by Javier taking Denise from Ant. Fuck them all. I hope they all leave here with more than what they came with and take whatever they get back to their baby mamas.

The pain they caused me in the past is not healable, even with me using revenge as a bandage. I missed prom because Keisha fucked Kevin, my boyfriend and prom date. I could never get back those years that they stole from me.

Almost an hour later, Amber knocked and said they were done. I woke the men up and showed them the door. Tyrone tried to play too high to drive and announced he would just roll out early. That wasn't in my plan. I still had shit to handle tonight, and I'd be damned before I'd sleep in a house full of lowlifes. Once I reminded them that Keisha and the girls have probably been looking for them all night, he agreed to leave.

As a friendly reminder, I told them they smelled like pussy, so maybe they should say they went to a cheap strip club. I had the women clean up my living room the best that they could.

April told me Tyrone was a nasty motherfucka and he nutted in her with no hesitation.

"Take some of the money I'm paying you and go get the morning-after pill . . . just in case."

She rejected my directions, informing me she couldn't get pregnant if someone paid her to. She'd had a hysterectomy at twenty-one years old.

Stephanie rode with me to drop the women back off on Sunset with their newly earned $1,500, clothes, and hairdos. They all thanked me, and then headed in their own directions to fight over johns. I wondered if any of them had ever been paid to do what they did tonight. In their line of work, I'm sure they have made money doing a lot worse.

We didn't go back to the rental property. We headed to Stephanie's house, which was closer to Hollywood than my house. On the ride there, Stephanie asked me how I was so sure it was going to work.

I responded honestly, even though I didn't explain what the truth was. All I said was, "It was that X factor," and broke out into laughter.

In the morning, we would send a cleaning crew to clean up last night's mess, and Stephanie will retrieve the tape once we got off of work. I should have my time-share sold in less than a week.

I was waiting to feel guilty about what I had done or some kind of remorse, but it wasn't there. The men are hoes, and so are their women. It was only right that I used hoes to belittle them all.

Tyrone's theory on the ride to get him something to eat had impacted my thoughts on life, karma, and fate. My plan worked too easily for it not to have been meant. There were no snags or shortcomings. Whatever happens after this weekend was meant to happen. It's a part of a plan that couldn't have been changed. I wouldn't face any repercussions for my actions tonight because I was the one who was chosen to help them meet their fate.

Fuck that . . . The truth was that I didn't give a fuck about them or their crazy lifelong relationships. I didn't care about their fate. I wanted five-star revenge, and I got it tonight, without breaking a sweat. That was proof that I only loved myself and . . . Dre.

I wouldn't admit it to myself, but he was right. There was something between us that I had never felt before, and I wasn't ready for it to end, but it had to.

For some reason, I felt my life was about to change, yet I couldn't determine in which direction it was headed. One thing I did know was it was time to fly out to Washington and find myself a new place to call home. After twelve years, I had finally gotten my revenge. Damn, did it feel good.

Chapter 13

The Perfect Getaway

Two months had passed since my little "house party" with the men. I was feeling renewed and alive. I was planning to have lunch with Stephanie and Erika.

Our new intern, Erika, was doing great, so I thought I'd schedule us lunch at Stevie's on the Strip, but had to cancel and set up an in-office lunch with them instead. I ordered Chinese food, and we sat on my rug and ate.

Erika had warmed up to us and started talking more. She was such a sweet girl. Her family put her older sister first and paid her no attention, so it became her goal to be the best at everything else and earn their attention. She didn't deal with her big sister at all, unless she was in trouble; then Erika would run to her rescue. Erika still believed that blood was thicker than water.

She wasn't related to Memphis, that's why. If Memphis was in trouble, he knew he couldn't count on me, and it was his fault we were like that.

During lunch, my phone went off, but it was just a text message. To my shock, it was Javier. The text read: Can you please give April my phone number? I'll travel to the South for her ass.

I almost pissed on myself from laughing. Stephanie had to read this shit. "Stephanie, why is your friend Javier texting me asking for April's number?"

She snatched my phone, and she fell out laughing too. Erika was looking at us both like we had lost our minds.

"Are y'all going to keep on laughing, or y'all going to let me in on it?"

I didn't see any harm in telling her bits and pieces of what happened. As long as I didn't make myself and Stephanie look bad, she could know. "I had these guys over to my house a few months back, and there were a few girls there we had just met too. The men got drunk out of their minds and had sex with all the women at my house, except Stephanie and myself. We told them to use a condom, but they refused to, and come to find out, the girls were prostitutes. I know it doesn't sound like something we should be laughing at, but these men and their baby mamas tormented me as a child. That has nothing to do with their karma, though. That was all fate."

I continued laughing, and so did Stephanie. Erika had a smile on her face, but I guess she would have to hear the whole story to laugh.

"This one has to go in the planner, the day Javier begged for more toxic pussy. I bet you Tyrone and Ant been thinking about them too."

I wrapped up lunch because I had to meet with a possible buyer on the time-share I was selling on Pacific Coast Highway. Stephanie also had to leave because it was her firefighter fuck day. We were leaving Erika in charge.

I was about fifteen minutes away from the time-share when I realized I didn't know my prospective buyer's name. It was in the planner, and Stephanie was gone for the day. Maybe I could get Erika to get it out of her office for me. I called the office and had the secretary transfer me to Erika's cubical. Instead, she transferred me to Stephanie's office. Apparently, Stephanie had left Erika some of her work to do.

"Erika, can you do me a favor, sweetheart? Look in Stephanie's top sliding drawer and pull out that black planner. Look up today's date and tell me the name of the person I'm supposed to meet, please." I didn't hear the drawer open, yet she was flipping through pages. "Did you find it?"

Her voice sounded slightly different when she spoke, kind of ghetto, to be exact. "Yep, I found it. She left it sitting on top of her desk. You supposed to meet with a Mr. P. Johns at 3:00 p.m."

I thanked her and told her I'd see her Monday, but she didn't let me get off the phone.

"Savannah, can I ask you a question? And please be honest. If something evil was happening to your sister, and you were the only person who could help her, would you? Or would you use that opportunity to get payback for her doing you wrong in the past?"

I actually thought about what she asked me before I answered. "Erika, fuck my sister. I would be getting my revenge."

She took a deep breath, and then said, "That's what makes us different," and hung up the phone.

Her scandalous-ass sister must need her help with something. I hope she makes the right choice.

When I made it to the house, I was the only person there. Mr. Johns must have been running late. I hadn't been in that house since the janitor service cleaned it. In the ad I placed in the newspaper, I left Stephanie's number to set up viewings with the property manager. There was no telling who had been in and out of the unit last month.

When I walked up the steps, I could smell food coming from some unit. Something about it was familiar, and it smelled really good. I turned the handle on the door and finally met up with "P. Johns."

Sitting on my dining-room table were four extralarge boxes of Papa John's pizza with a note taped to the lid that read, *Veggie pizza, add Chicken.*

I ran through each room looking for Dre while screaming his name. He wasn't in the house or anywhere nearby. This was his way of letting me know he was out, back on the streets, and in or on his way to California. The game of cat and mouse or hide-and-go-seek was about to start, and my first hiding spot would be in Washington. I would leave California no later than Tuesday.

I flew home. I hit 120 mph all the way there, turning a fifteen- or twenty-minute drive into a seven-minute one. Dre had detective friends, and I didn't want to make myself look obvious. I stayed in the house for about five hours before leaving with all the jewelry and belongings that would fit in my Dolce bag.

This place was paid for until six months from now, so there was no rush to move my stuff. I would wait until I was settled to have my daddy and uncle pack up my stuff.

I was moving so fast and didn't have anywhere to go. Stephanie was somewhere being fucked until Saturday, and I couldn't go stay at my daddy's house due to where it was located. Then I got my destination. Will called to see if I could be his partner for a two-on-two charity basketball fundraiser that was being thrown by the California Department of Sheriffs in San Francisco.

"I know it's last minute, but they are short a team from the Los Angeles County Sheriff's Department, and I was asked to save the day. I could have called another girl, but I decided I wanted to win, and you became my first choice."

To get the hell away from Dre, I would have volunteered to play basketball naked in the snow with some Timberland boots on and a cowboy hat.

"Sure, I'll do it. It's for charity, and my company will make a large donation. Where should we meet?"

He asked if I could meet him at his job to sign up, and we would then take a flight out at seven o'clock in the morning. The game wasn't until eight o'clock Saturday night, but he wanted us to get there early enough to get in some practice and get a feel of each other's game.

I agreed and headed straight to the sheriff's office. Now, let's see Dre and his goons follow me in there.

When I arrived, he told me that he booked us flights out of Burbank airport in the morning. I mentioned how I would have to get up at 3:30 just to make sure I was up and at the airport by 6:00 a.m. When he heard that, he invited me to stay at his house. Now, that was real protective custody.

"Do you need to go home and pack?"

I put a big smile on my face. "No, I have everything I need on me. I plan to go pick up something on the way to your house."

He wrote his address down and gave me his spare key. "I don't get off for another hour or so. Make yourself at home. There's nothing in the fridge, but we'll go out to dinner later on tonight."

The address he gave me was near the post office my PO Box was at. I hadn't checked it in almost four months. It was packed with a large envelope that had a DVD and birthday party pictures. Dre's genes were strong because my daughter was his female twin. She looked exactly like her father with dimples. No one in my family has dimples, so they must have come from Dre's side of the gene pool.

In the pictures, there must have been fifty or more guests and a mountain of gifts for Sade. The letter said they opened a banking account for her with the $3,000 I sent her for her birthday. I was glad about the decision I made to give her up. I would have never been able to get a house full of people to gather like that for her third birthday. Knowing me, we would have gone to Hawaii or somewhere to celebrate it alone or with her nanny.

The DVD must be a recording of her party because they sent one on her first and second birthday too. I hoped Will has a DVD player. I couldn't wait to hear her talk and see her in action.

When I made it to Will's house, I was shocked at how beautiful it was. The color threw me for a loop. Everything was a soft lilac purple. You never see men take the time to fully decorate, and it was a work of art. He had handwoven drapes with expensive scarves over all his windows, beautiful black empowerment artwork everywhere, and his bathroom was covered in beautiful purple lilies. He must have had a woman living with him previously, because I snooped around, but there was nothing in the house that could be owned by a woman.

I made myself comfortable on the couch and popped in the DVD. Sade was walking and talking like a big girl now. The Jeffersons had her blowing me kisses and telling me that she loved me. It was the cutest thing. Sade grabbed the video camera and kissed it. When they tried to take it from her, she started screaming, "Mama, Mama, help."

At end of the video, they asked if I would send a picture for Sade's purposes. It was Mr. Jefferson's request. "I know you don't want nobody to know who you are and all that good stuff, but little Sade knows she has a mother out there, and it would be a beautiful thing if she knew what her mother looked like. That's just my suggestion."

I wouldn't kick the thought out completely, but with Dre playing detective, now wasn't the best time. As I was replaying the part when Sade started screaming "Mama," the owner of the house caught me red-handed.

"Whose baby girl is that?" Will asked, and then waited on my answer.

"My little goddaughter. Isn't she the prettiest little thing?" He agreed while I rushed to take it out of the DVD player and placed it back in its envelope to go stash in my car.

"Well, Ms. Savannah, are you ready to go eat?"

I snatched my purse and package up and said, "Sure."

We decided to go Cheesecake Factory so we could walk out with a three-layered strawberry cheesecake, which was my request. While we waited for our food to be served, I sparked up the conversation.

"Who decorated your place? It's beautiful. I had thought about hiring an interior decorator, but decided to wait until I was permanently parked somewhere. I move too much and leave too much behind when I do move to waste money like that."

He smiled shyly. "Thank you. I did hire an interior decorator, or I should say, I am dating one. My baby said my place looked too masculine and gave off the wrong vibe about me. So, I agreed to the update."

I knew it. That house had been touched by a woman. The only way he would have convinced me that he did all that himself was if he was gay, and Will was far from gay.

"Keep dating her, 'cause I may need her. I'm moving away from California next week, and this might be my last move." With Sade being so close and me being a partner at the firm and the head over our West Coast operations, Washington wasn't looking so bad after all.

"I'm sorry. I didn't know you were moving. If you need to stay and pack or something, I'll understand."

What he didn't know was that with Dre on the loose, he was my new security guard. I wasn't leaving his side until Monday.

"No, I'm fine. I sent all my stuff ahead. All I have left in California is my car and everything in this purse."

I needed to arrange for Stephanie to follow me in her car as I sold both of my vehicles on Monday. I might have changed the plates, but the VIN numbers stayed the same. That might be how Dre tracked me down. I'd get something new when I made it to Washington.

Once we were full, we headed back to Will's to get some rest before the flight. I really wanted him to fuck me, but was thankful he hadn't tried. There was no way I could be a good sex partner with Dre on my mind.

The flight to San Francisco was beautiful. I hadn't flown since I moved from Atlanta. We found a NIKE shop where I got my game supplies, basketball, tennis shoes, shorts, sports bra, wristbands, and all.

After an hour of practice, I knew I still had it, and this tournament would be ours—and it was. We took first place without breaking a sweat. We left with the first-place trophy and ribbons, which would be placed at the Los Angeles Sheriff Department's main hub, but that was nice of them to let Will leave with it.

A few of his coworkers invited us out to a strip club to celebrate, but he turned them down, saying, "I've never hung with them fake-ass niggas. They just want to be nosy and find out who you are."

If I wasn't trying to get some of Will's dick, I wouldn't have minded getting to know any of them. They all were sexy.

"Well, let's have our own celebration. Let's kill the liquor store and head back to the hotel and chill all night. Our flight doesn't leave 'til tomorrow night, and if we are hungover in the morning, we got a few hours before the trip home to recover."

Will was with it. We bought a big bottle of tequila and went to work on it. We both were drunk because we started being open about everything and eventually crossed the privacy lines.

"Savannah, I miss my boo. This is the longest we've been apart in nine months and it's killing me. I keep having 'what if there's some cheating going on' thoughts, which ain't cool. I know my baby loves me, but damn, it's hard. I feel so safe and protected when my baby is around, and I got a gun at my waist and the other on my ankle all day, and I don't feel as protected as I do when my boo boo's here. It's like nothing even matters. Now that we're apart, I keep checking my phone for texts or missed calls. This feels like high school again."

Blame it on the alcohol, but I couldn't bite my tongue. "Your boo is a man, huh? You're gay. I knew it! Well, I didn't know it, but your house gave a hint of it, and I didn't see any women's belongings lying around. Yet you had two different brands of deodorant on your bathroom sink and two toothbrushes."

He confirmed my suspicion and made me vow not to tell anyone. No one knew but him and his boo, Alvin. I felt privileged being his secret holder and decided to make him mine. "The little girl in the video is my daughter. She's three years old, and her name is Sade." I went through the same spiel about no one knowing and how I've wanted to get it off my chest. I told him about Dre, the pizza, and everything. Then he let me in on the biggest secret of the night.

Tyrone was in jail getting head from a nigga who went around saying he could predict the future and take a glimpse into people's fate. Will said Tyrone didn't know that he knew, but he confirmed it was true.

He arranged for the dude to meet them at the courts one night, and he said, "Tyrone looked like he was going to shit on himself. When his past lover walked his way, Tyrone grabbed his shit and left. I had stopped fucking with Tyrone way before this because he tried to blame me for the way his life turned out. He said he couldn't get out of the game because I introduced him to it, and now I hide behind a badge. I tried to let him know he was talking stupid by saying he was a follower of somebody three years younger than he was, but fuck him. Next time he goes to jail, I hope he gets his dick sucked by one of them AIDS-having niggas in there—unless his ex-man taught him how to predict the future too."

I hit the floor laughing. Will was now my new homegirl. I mean homeboy. Fuck it. He was my new bitch and my secret keeper.

On the flight back home to Los Angles, we held hands the whole way as we talked about everybody on the plane like only true bitches would.

Chapter 14

Sister to Sister

Monday morning, I was up and on the telephone with Stephanie before she dressed for work. I told her all about Dre's delivery setup at the time-share.

"Why didn't you call me, Savannah? You know I would have been on my way. Why is this nigga so attached to you? I could see if y'all would have been talking marriage or if you had his child, but this stalking and following you shit is crazy. Did you tell the police?"

How do you tell the police that you have a stalker when you're hiding the stalker's child? "No, I didn't tell the police. I booked a flight to Washington tomorrow, and I'm gone. Fuck California. I got my revenge, the company is running fine, and I have no ties here. I'll still be close to my daddy, and he can visit anytime. It's time to settle down in a new place. When you're done fighting fires with your man, I'll be up north waiting on you."

Stephanie said she would be right behind me in two weeks. She would start preparing herself for the move. Not being conceited, but I knew that would be her response. As far as family was concerned, I was all she had, and she wasn't going to let me move on without her.

We met up at Clifton's in downtown LA for breakfast. My daddy used to take Memphis and me there every weekend as children. The restaurant wasn't as well-kept as it was back then, but the food was still good. I wrapped my toast in my napkin and headed out the door to sell my cars.

Fifteen thousand dollars was what I made from the Charger, and another $10,000 for the 300. It was hard selling my babies.

Starting all over was going to be hard too. There are fifty states in the United States, and I have been banned from three of them. The only thing that could bring me back to Georgia, California, or Tennessee was my job and my daddy, and I would try hard to make both things come to me.

I told my uncle Johnny I was leaving first. He was saddened by my news, but knew I had a career and my own life to live. Next, I called my daddy and told him.

"Daddy, in two weeks, I need you to go close that PO Box for me. If there's anything in it, don't open it. Just mail it to me in Washington. If Keisha or any of them start looking for me or start asking for me, tell them I'm back in the South and please, don't tell Memphis where I am. Let him think I'm in the South too."

He cut me off. "There's a lot of talk going around here with your name in it, Savannah. I think it's time I move away from here too. I'm getting too old to be in the middle of stuff. Don't worry about what's going on and what's being said. Just sell this house like you're doing yours. Yes, mine's too, and find me an apartment in Washington. Memphis has moved away with some girl in Moreno Valley until he can find him a place. I don't know what the problem is between you and him, but you need to know your brother loves you."

There wasn't nothing I could say but, "Yes, Daddy. I'll get you out of there in three days." He said he was headed to Johnny's house and would get the PO Box transferred to Seattle.

The office was closed for the day, but I would make sure to call Stephanie after my flight landed tomorrow for a checkup on things. I had stayed my last night as a Californian with Will and Alvin.

"Your baby daddy was released about a year ago, but was on six months' probation, which he completed in four months. He was a hard man to trace with Nashville detectives helping to clean up his footsteps, but I got him. His last known whereabouts were in Las Vegas. He rented a car there about five months ago, and I bet you were there with Ant that weekend too. You're wondering how he knew where you were going, I bet. Well, that was easy when he has yours and Stephanie's office lines tapped. You ain't messing with no fool, girl, so be careful in Washington. You're the only best friend I got and I don't want to lose my job hurting somebody over you, okay?"

I zoned out after Vegas. Dre was the purchaser of my flower at the club. He has been close enough to confront me on many occasions, so why hadn't he? What was he waiting on?

I couldn't sleep that night. I stayed up watching the news. There was a report of a small earthquake, which I didn't feel, as usual. It was reported to have been 4.0 in magnitude, which meant if I was walking, I wouldn't have felt it. Let me know when it's larger than 6.0.

My Al Green ringtone was going off, so I knew it was my daddy calling me to see if I was safe. "I didn't feel it, Daddy, and, yes, I'm safe. Go back to sleep."

All I could hear coming from his end of the phone was loud sirens—both police and fire trucks. "Savannah, what did you do, baby? They have burnt down the house. Everything my mama worked hard for just burnt up in my face, and I can't stop it. The police want you to meet them at the station to question you."

I was speechless and scared. I didn't know what to say but, "What do they want to question me for, Daddy?"

He was crying, and I could hear it in his voice. "Baby, whoever it was that did this to the house wants you. They spray-painted your name all over the house and put, 'Come get your revenge, bitch' on the ground in the driveway. I'm worried about you. Please meet these policemen for help."

I agreed and told him to meet me down there. I woke up my new best friend and told him what went down. I told him to cancel my flight, even though it may have been best that I did leave California now. However, I wasn't going to leave my daddy alone.

The police station was packed when I arrived. I had taken Alvin's car since he was off work today. I made it there at 4:00 a.m. but didn't speak with a detective until 7:00 a.m.

"Mrs. James, why do you think this group of women that you named would have burned down your father's house?"

My answer was embarrassing, but it was the truth. "They did it because I fucked all three of their baby daddies over the last six months."

We talked for two hours; then she took me into a room where she had all three women in a lineup with three other women. I pointed out Keisha, Christina, and Melinda, and then I left. The detective asked me not to leave the state for at least seventy-two hours just in case I was needed to come back down.

I called Stephanie, told her what happened, and had her meet me at Will's house to take Alvin's car back. We went straight to the office to make sure everything was fine, plus, I kept an emergency business suit there just in case my partners showed up unannounced. I needed to change clothes badly.

Our office bathroom was large enough for me to wash up really well and fix my hair and face. Thank God for miniflatirons. I kept a pair in my desk drawer.

When I was done, Stephanie was in her office reading over a handwritten letter. When I asked what it was, she said she was sorry and handed it to me.

To Whom It May Concern:

This is my written resignation from my internship with Williams and Williamson. My reason for leaving is entirely personal. I am glad I was made aware of the drama and games that are played by the heads of this company and have decided I want no part of it, especially when the victim is my sister and her friends. I know this letter is being read by either Stephanie or Savannah's trifling ass, so I'm done with the professional half of it. You bitches better pray my sister and her child's father don't get anything more than the flu, or you will have to deal with me. I did make my sister aware that Savannah fucked Tyrone, Javier, and Ant, but I haven't told her about the orgy you had at your house with all of your friends. Savannah, you're a nasty bitch and you better pray you have a clean bill of health.

Erika Soto,

Keisha Soto's baby sister.

Before I could ask Stephanie, she answered. "The planner is gone, and, no, I didn't put the ladies were prostitutes in the book. We laughed about it in her face. We only said Javier's name. I'm sorry, Savannah, I fucked up."

Fucked up was putting it nicely. She had ruined everything with that *Kill Bill* notepad she kept. I could kick her ass for this. My family lost a house that they had been there for years, my daddy was now homeless, and everybody wanted a piece of me. No one cared about Stephanie's involvement. *I* was the one who fucked up. They wanted me.

"Hey, Will, you got a minute? I need your help." I told Will I needed him to get all six of their whereabouts.

Will suggested my father and I stay with him, which was in protective custody until we left for Washington. I had no choice but to agree.

I had finally calmed myself down when I was hit with the next piece of news. I got a call from the Santa Monica Fire Department telling me that my time-share had just gone up in smoke. I should thank them because it became hard to sell. I would get insurance money instead, which was fine with me, and with all the women in jail, it left the men as suspects.

As I was looking for the detective's number I had spoken to this morning to tell her what happened to my unit, Will called back. "Okay, boo, Keisha, Melinda, and Christina are still locked up at the police subdivision, and they all are going to be on probation, so don't worry about them moving anytime soon. Ant is back at school and has been there for about a month.

That was confirmed by his basketball coach. And Tyrone and Javier are riding around handling some business for their babies' mamas. I played like I didn't know shit and was told to be careful, that you are a sick ho on the loose, and they are going to 'teach you a lesson.'"

When I told Will my house was on fire, he told me to report it to the detective so I could have Tyrone and Javier picked up for questioning. I told him I would, thanked him for all his help, and told him I'd see him later.

Uncle Johnny waited three days after the fire, and then went by my house in Malibu. Surprisingly, it hadn't been touched, and that was because no one knew about it. That house was in Uncle Johnny's name, and right now, I was glad it was because I wanted to bathe at my own place and change my clothes where I had a larger variety. Everything in my bathroom, kitchen, and linen closet had been packed in forty-five minutes. The TVs and furniture I gave to my uncle Steve as a shut-the-fuck-up gift.

He had called talking shit yesterday about the house getting burned down and mentioned something about Memphis.

"This shit is all of your fault. When are you moving back to Georgia? I need you to leave the state before you fuck my life up next. First, my mama's house, and now Memphis. Where's my lucky rabbit's foot at? You need to get baptized soon!"

I had yet to find out what Memphis had done to make him flee the way he did. Whatever it was, my daddy knew he couldn't come back to LA.

I had given the detectives longer than seventy-two hours. I stayed there a whole week. My daddy still had to wait for his insurance check, and he wouldn't be flying out for another week, which was perfect because it gave me time to find him a new house instead of an apartment and deck it out.

Stephanie left with me. She found her a place not too far from mine in Seattle. Even with Tyrone, Javier, Keisha, Melinda, and Christina in jail, she was still scared. Stephanie was worried about Erika and Ant. Ant was smart. He wouldn't do anything stupid while his crew was in jail because he didn't want to join them.

My concern was that bitch, Erika. I didn't know her like I knew the others. To be honest, after this week, I realized I didn't know them, either.

***

It was raining when we made it to Seattle and it was a lot colder than California. Stephanie rented a car and dropped me off at my new home in northern Seattle, which I was told was where the business class lived.

I was purchasing a three-bedroom, two-bath-room house with an underground pool and Jacuzzi for $725,000. Since I was purchasing and not renting, Mr. Nguyen gave me a check for $100,000 toward the purchase of my home, which I was thankful for because, technically, he didn't have to. The new Seattle office is to service other clients since the California location was dedicated to Strax Industries. My move doesn't benefit Mr. Nguyen in any form, but he felt the need to help since he had gotten me to leave Georgia.

The house was huge and empty. After I found my daddy a place, I would go car and furniture shopping. For now, I would enjoy my alone time and get some sleep. I woke up to Stephanie ringing my doorbell like she had lost her mind.

"I'm not staying in that house by myself yet. It's raining too hard." She pushed past me and sat on my living-room floor.

"After we get this weed in our system, you got to show me around. This place is huge."

How in the hell did Stephanie get some weed already? We had only been here six hours.

"Don't underestimate me, Savannah; I see how you're looking at me." She spread her legs, dug in her pants, and came out with a condom full of weed.

"You know I had to find a way to get some California weed to Washington." She reached into her purse, pulled out two blunts, and said, "Here's to starting over."

We smoked both blunts back-to-back, and I was out. I hadn't had any sleep in days, so I needed the rest. I dreamed about Dre and I meeting up at a hotel somewhere in New York because I could see a little of Time's Square from my hotel's view.

We started off arguing over Sade and her best interests regarding her parenting. Dre had won the dispute, as usual, and we were now lip-locked, rolling around the bed, and competing on who could take the other's clothes off first. It was abusive sex. There was a lot of biting, scratching, slapping, and spanking going on from both of us. He bit my shoulder and flipped me on top of him in a saddle position. I slapped his face and covered it with my breasts. Slowly, he gripped my sides, squeezing as hard as he could until I closed my eyes from the pain.

When I opened my eyes, there was Keisha standing in front of me with a gun pointed at my face. Before I could beg for my life, she pulled the trigger.

I woke up covered in sweat. I didn't mean to startle Stephanie, but I needed some fresh air. I asked if we could drive around looking for a place for my dad, and then go get some dinner. It was five o'clock in the afternoon and nothing seemed to close until 8:00 or 9:00 p.m. here.

I found my daddy a place in between Stephanie's and mine. It was a nice-sized two-bedroom, two-bathroom house with a nice-sized backyard and garage. I signed a two-year lease on the house and paid off the first year up front. There wasn't a background check or credit check done at all. The owner had me complete an application, and when I asked if I could pay a year in advance, he was handing me the keys. Money talks, bullshit walks, and it was evident in this situation.

We made it to Ashley Furniture by 7:30 p.m., and I had my daddy's entire place furnished. I even bought Memphis a king-sized bed, just in case he moved here.

There was a Lowes across from the furniture store. I ordered my daddy a new stainless steel stove and refrigerator and would have it and his cabinets packed with food before he got here. All I needed to get him was two TVs, one for the living room, the other for the bedroom, and an entertainment system to play his oldies on. This was the least I could do after what I let happen to his mother's house. I didn't want any of my insurance money I got from my unit. I would spend it all on him. There was a twenty-four-hour Walmart we passed on the way here where I got the TVs and a few other homely items on our way home.

I told Stephanie to pull into a gas station so I could get a map. The car she rented didn't come with GPS and was in need of a new pair of windshield wipers badly. It sounded as if they were scratching the window. As I was bending over the car to put the new wipers on, this sexy-ass, green-eyed white man took them from me and put them on. When he was done, I introduced myself.

"Thank you for your help. But I could have done it. My name is Savannah, and yours?"

He handed me his business card. It read: *Wayne Jacob Junior of Jacob's Cadillac.*

"Is it your car lot or your father's, Junior?"

He was amused. I could see it in his smile. "My father has been dead for the last five years. It's mine now."

I had never thought about owning a Cadillac before, but now I knew it was going to be the next vehicle I purchased.

"I hope you come by so we can talk about windshield wipers and things of that nature." He had the nerve to be flirting too.

"I'll see you tomorrow around noon. Maybe we can have that discussion over lunch."

Wayne agreed and planned to meet at 12:30 p.m. Before I let him go, I needed one more thing from him. "How do I get to the Jefferson's family restaurant in Tacoma from here?"

Chapter 15

Trial by Jury

It was nine at night, and the restaurant was packed with people. When we walked in, the smell was warming, and I was ready to eat. We sat opposite a live jazz band that didn't have a singer. The sound was relaxing, yet it was a rhythm you could dance to, and there was a floor full of people dancing. One thing I noticed was there were no alcoholic beverages on the menu. When they said family, they meant it.

A girl no more than the age of sixteen asked what we would like to drink. We both ordered strawberry lemonades.

"Savannah, this place is nice. How did you hear about it?"

I lied, of course, saying I went to school with someone whose family owned it. Glancing at the menu, I saw that there was a section on it that read, *Don't worry about pleasing the scale, please your soul.* From the heading, I knew that was where my meal was coming from. I ordered turkey necks with rice and brown gravy, collard greens, sweet potatoes, and corn bread with honey butter. Stephanie ordered smothered pork chops with mashed potatoes, cabbage, and a side of dressing, with a roll.

The food was awesome. It was on Georgia's level when it came to judging soul food. The Jeffersons had to be Southerners.

Peach cobbler and vanilla ice cream is what I ordered for dessert, and Stephanie ordered pecan pie. The best part of the night was when our bill was brought to us. The owner and the head chef delivered our bill with their beautiful daughter, Sade.

"How was everything?" Mrs. Jefferson asked.

I was in such a trance from staring at Sade, I almost didn't answer. "It was perfect. I lived in the South for eight years and have never seen, I mean, tasted, anything like it." I kept my eye on Sade the entire time. Mrs. Jefferson was explaining that she was born in Mississippi and fell in love with a soldier who wanted to take over his family business one day, and that's how she ended up here.

"Savannah, quit staring at that baby like that. I hope you're not getting baby blues. We both know you don't need any children."

I didn't pay Stephanie any mind. I reached out for Sade, and she came right to me, just like she did at the hospital. No fussing or nothing.

"You are pretty," Sade said while holding my face. I didn't know how to respond.

"Well, thank you very much. You are pretty too, and I love your hair."

Mrs. Jefferson reached for Sade, and she went to her. "I'm sorry about my goddaughter. She is such a friendly girl. She talks to every customer who comes in and out of here. Excuse me."

Mrs. Jefferson headed back to the kitchen, but Mr. Jefferson didn't move an inch. He grabbed the bill and ripped it up. "Y'all have a nice night."

Stephanie stood up. "Oh no, sir, after that meal, we *have* to pay. It was better than my mama's—don't tell her I said it, though."

He pushed her hand away from her purse and looked me dead in the eyes. "I know old family when I see it. This was better than any picture that could be sent. Y'all have a good night."

He turned his head and headed in his wife's direction, more than likely to tell her who I was. I jumped up quickly, grabbed Stephanie, and left a $1,000 tip.

"What are you smiling about, Savannah? You've had that smile on your face since we left the restaurant."

I ignored her all the way home, and when we got back to my house, I made her roll up, and then I went to sleep, nightmare free.

I was enjoying my new Cadillac DTS. It only cost me $20,000 in cash and about three days of boring-ass sex from Wayne.

My street should have been named Bayside because I was saved by the bell, commonly known as Bella Jacob, Wayne Jacob Junior's wife. The Jacobs lived four houses down from mine with their son, Winston. Bella was a part of the welcoming committee in my subdivision, and she and her family knocked on my door to welcome me to the neighborhood. Wayne looked sick when I answered the door, but I saved his ass.

"Hello there, Mr. Jacobs, I love my new Cadillac. Bella, your husband here gave me such a good deal, I couldn't say no."

Since our little family meeting, he hadn't picked up the phone to call me. How lucky could I get?

My daddy was supposed to be here over four months ago, but couldn't make the flight. He made it all the way to check-in before he realized he was afraid to fly. In almost fifty-five years, this man had never been on a plane.

I had built up the courage to fly down to get him, and then drive seventeen hours back to Seattle so he could finally stay at his own place. The drive wasn't going to be the worst part of it. Memphis had been staying with my uncle too, so I would be in his presence all those hours as well. I wanted to bring Stephanie with me badly, but I needed her to get groceries for my daddy's place so he and Memphis would feel at home when they made it. I even got Memphis a PlayStation 3 with all the games he used to have at home. I bet they play well on the fifty-two-inch TV I put in his room.

When I made it to the airport, I called my daddy to let him know I'd be there in about four hours and to meet me at the office with their stuff. He was trying to tell me something about the PO Box, but Will was buzzing in so I had to go.

"Don't leave me waiting on you at airport, bestie. You know I got people who want to hurt me out there." Will was going to pick me up in my rental car, and then I'd drop him back off at the sheriff's station.

"Bitch, please, you got angels around. You want the news now or later? And if your impatient ass says now, what news you want first? Good, bad, or weird?"

Talking to Will was really like talking to a woman. I don't see how he controlled cutting it off during work hours. He was a natural bitch.

"Start with the weird, then give me the bad, and end with some good. How about that?"

He took a deep breath, and then started running his mouth. "Erika, the bitch's sister, turned herself in and took all the credit for what Keisha had done. She said it was her, Christina, and Melinda, who had burnt down your daddy's house, and that Keisha had no part of it. The bitch had priors as a minor; remember when she stabbed her daddy, and they put her in Juvenile Hall for four years? Or was you already gone then? Anyway, the bitch is looking at five to seven years for arson, plus her priors. We won't see her for about ten years, and when she does get released, she will be under the care of a psychiatrist.

"Now for the bad news: Keisha may be walking the streets in less than a year. Since her sister took all the credit, she is only in jail for a probation violation for being in contact with other people on probation. That sucks, don't it? The state took TJ, and he will be calling somebody else Mama and Daddy until she gets her shit straight. The good side of this is Keisha was removed from general population and put on the med list, and so was her baby daddy. Can you say *HIV-positive?* It gets worse for Tyrone, though. Him and Javier played baseball, baby, and they both struck out. Two newcomers to the California three strikes law—bye-bye, bitches. Ant wanted me to tell you that he was sorry about your daddy's house. The big idiot thinks everybody flipped out over you fucking everybody. I guess Erika kept her word and kept it to herself. There you go, beautiful. You are good to walk the streets of LA again, and I will get you a release date on Keisha tomorrow. Now, get your sexy ass on the plane, bitch, and I'll see you in two hours and thirty minutes. Kisses."

I had really gotten my revenge . . . and won. Yes, it cost my family their house, but look at the outcome for everybody else. Two of them were lifers, two had HIV, and in the next six months, others may have the same diagnosis. Two had fifteen years, one had ten, and as for Ant . . . I had never wanted him hurt to begin with.

I couldn't wait to knock out this seventeen-hour drive home just to go home and celebrate. Nothing in this world could take this feeling away from me.

I asked the stewardess for a cup of water so I could take my daily BC Powder for the pains I still had in my upper hip/lower stomach, and I smiled all the way to LAX.

Will was at the airport holding a welcome home sign for me at the baggage claim. I was glad I had a real friend like him. There was Sandy, but if I didn't pick up the phone, she didn't call, and Stephanie was my girl because we still worked together, but there was a lot about me she didn't know. I had only been real friends with Will for five months, although I've known him my entire life, and he knew about Sade. I couldn't wait to tell him what happened at the restaurant.

"Why are you trying to make me cry? I want a picture of my god-baby. Promise me you're going to get her back once you settle your hot ass down, or at least let her meet you. You shouldn't do that baby like your mama did you. That ain't right, and you know that shit."

For the last year, I've been so scared of the Hoes Crew I wasn't the evil bitch I used to be and I didn't feel like going back and being her either. Meeting Dre showed me that love could come easy and seeking revenge taught me that being evil took hard work, a lot of time, and you can lose yourself on the journey to get it. I was lost and no one would want me to be found because I fucked over everyone that came near me. My daughter wasn't excluded. After all the hell I caused, I'd witness enough. I wasn't worried about karma. My decision to start over and try to live my life right was because I had gotten the chip off my shoulder that had been there since thirteen. Why strive to be a bitch when there wasn't any anger, hurt, or embarrassment left to fuel it? I'm done because it's done.

"I'm not going to promise you nothing, but I will keep it in mind."

We hugged, kissed, and said our good-byes. Will promised he and Alvin were going to fly out to Seattle in three months to see me.

Williams and Williamson's was packed when I walked in. I almost forgot I was the head of the company until, one by one, people started kissing my ass.

"Continue working. This is not a pop-up visit. Those will be done by Stephanie. I'm just here to pick up my daddy. Everybody here does an outstanding job. I'm not worried about you at all."

The front-desk secretary told me that they were waiting for me in the large conference room and that I had a call, but when she put the person on hold, they had hung up.

When she said, "they," I never imagined that would include Dre. He was sitting in the middle of my daddy and my brother when I walked in the room. I turned my back and thought about walking out, but it was time to face Dre too.

"Dre, what the fuck are you doing here with my daddy and my brother? What the fuck is wrong with you?" I locked the door and moved closer to the center of the room.

Memphis stood up and moved his chair in front of the door, I guess to block me from leaving. "Sis, I don't know what happened or what's been going on over the last few years, but after I pulled my heat out on Tyrone, this man came to my rescue. He came looking for Daddy, but he wasn't there; then Tyrone pulled up talking about how you fucked and sucked him and his boys like a porno star—sorry, Daddy. I know we don't get along like that, but you my sister and you doing good for yourself. I wasn't going to let a nigga disrespect you like that, so I pulled out my heat; then Tyrone and Javier pulled out theirs, and that's when that man there jumped in between all of us and snatched me up. Savannah, just hear the nigga out. He didn't say shit to me . . . just dropped me off at Uncle Steve's house."

I was touched that Memphis had tried to be a brother, but he didn't know the history between Dre and me. When my daddy spoke up, I felt the pains in my side increase.

"I went to go and close that PO Box today, and I took this envelope out of it. This man here watched me as I did it, and then came up to me and begged me to open it up in front of you and him together. Savannah, you know I don't play games and, lately, you have put me in a lot of the games you decided to play with people's lives. Now, I'm going to give you a chance to tell your side of whatever it is that's going on between you and Andre, and if you don't tell me, then I will listen to his side and believe everything this man says—now choose."

I snatched a chair from under the table and sat down. My phone started ringing back-to-back. It was Will, but I couldn't answer in the middle of this shit.

"Do what he says, Daddy. Open the envelope in front of both of us."

My daddy opened the envelope and there was an 8x10 inch photo of Sade. Dre stood up and stared at it. I watched the tears come pouring out of his eyes, and they started coming out of mine too. My daddy looked at the picture, and then looked at both of us back and forth. Memphis walked over and looked at the picture.

"Man, she looks just like you, but I don't get it. Why my sister got a picture of your baby coming to a PO Box she set up in my daddy's name?"

My daddy was far from being stupid. He answered Memphis's question without confirmation from Dre or me. "That's because she's your niece. She is Savannah's baby."

He wiped his eyes and started shaking his head. Memphis went and stood by Dre. "Is that my niece? Where she at? Savannah, where your daughter at? One of y'all needs to speak up." Memphis started balling up his fists and getting louder with his questions.

It was time for me to face my past. Dre proved I couldn't hide from him forever. "Yes, that is your niece. Her name is Sade, and she'll be four in three and a half months. She lives thirty minutes from us in Tacoma, Washington, with her foster parents, and Dre is her father. I fell in love with Dre, but he turned out to be a local thug, and when I found out I was pregnant by him, it was too late for an abortion, so I gave her away. Are you happy now, Dre? The truth is finally out."

I grabbed my phone that was still ringing off the hook and headed for the door. When I looked back, Memphis was patting my daddy on the back, and Dre was still holding Sade's picture.

"Daddy and Memphis, when y'all are ready to go, I'll be downstairs in a blue Nissan waiting on you. Dre, if you want to talk more about this, we can, but not in my place of business. Exchange numbers with my daddy or my brother and call me when you're ready." I walked out the door with my head high and answered Will's call as I headed out of the lobby to the parking garage.

"I ran into Mrs. Soto up here at the county jail putting money on Erika's books. She told me Keisha got out of jail last week, but will be right back in 'cause she promises to get you. Her mama said she has been calling your office from a payphone outside of your job every day, waiting on somebody to say you're there. I'm on my way, baby. Stay inside until I get there."

Will was already too late. When I walked outside to the rental car, Keisha had followed me right out the front door of the lobby in my office. I was all alone. I walked to the side of the building where I knew there was video surveillance with an armed security guard watching, but with how long it would take him to get here, I'd probably be dead.

Keisha was still far enough away from me to try to run, so I tried to run to the other side of the car. I heard six shots, then *click, click*. She ran out of bullets, but she didn't need any more. I'd been hit.

I didn't know where I was shot. I just hit the floor while Keisha went to work on me. I curled my arms around my face to protect it as I felt her kick me all over my body. She stomped on my rib cage over and over again while yelling, "Bitch, you thought you could get away with fucking my man? You thought I wouldn't find out? This is for me, Christina, and Melinda, bitch!"

Keisha dragged me by my legs closer to the car, grabbed a handful of my hair, and tried to slam my face into the door. It didn't work because my arms were covering it, but she did manage to slam the back of my head into the ground.

That's when the darkness came. I just closed my eyes and prayed that after the darkness, there would be a light. I prayed that when she was done, I would be able to open my eyes again, at least long enough to tell my daddy and Memphis that I was sorry and also to tell Dre I was sorry and that I did indeed love him. I loved him back then, and I still did.

I heard voices.

"Get the fuck off of her!"

Was that Memphis? It was too youthful to be my daddy's voice. Maybe it was Dre . . . Maybe he still loved me too.

Someone was yelling and another voice was screaming,

"Call 911, she's dying!"

There was a lot of whistling in the wind around me. Someone must have been wrestling. Keisha's grip on my hair was loosening, yet everything kept getting darker. Somebody had saved me. I just hope I lived to find out who it was.

Chapter 16

Deep Sleep

Where in the fuck am I? I keep hearing beeping and something was holding my eyes closed. It felt like tape when I finally got it off.

I was in a hospital, but a hospital where? I reached for the nurse button, but there was a nurse already in my room asleep. I couldn't use my voice. My mouth felt like it was stuffed with cotton. So I started shaking my bed to get her attention.

She woke up and flew to my bed. "Oh, Savannah, I'm so glad you woke up." She hit the nurse's button and yelled, "She's awake," and when my room filled with doctors and nurses, she disappeared.

It took three hours to get my voice back. It was more of a whisper, but at least it was something. Memphis and my daddy came running in my room.

"How are you feeling, baby? I knew you were going to wake up from that dream eventually."

Memphis kissed my forehead and said, "If you scare us again like that, I'm going to kill you myself."

I mustered up enough energy to ask, "Where am I, and what happened?"

Daddy told me that I had been shot in the back of my leg by Keisha and suffered a brain injury, which caused me to be in a slight coma for a few months. I was at the University of Washington Medical Center in Tacoma, Washington. I was transferred here at Dre's request.

"Daddy, why did you let that man decide where I needed to be? That's *your* decision."

He shook his head. "Savannah, you remind me of your mother so much. I know I never told you this, but you're just like her. Fussing for no reason, always trying to be in control. You know what else you're doing like her? You're trying to run off a good man who loves you and little Sade."

I had forgotten he had known about Sade and the secrets I was planning to take with me to the grave. "Savannah, before you were released from the hospital in California to be transferred to Washington, they told us you had cervical cancer. Dre went crazy, crying and screaming.

He almost got kicked out of the hospital. After doing some research, he found out this was one of the number one cancer centers in the United States and requested you be transferred here. That's why I let him decide. After all you have done to this man and, yes, he told me the whole story, he still loves you and wants to have a family with you."

Dre still loved me? I knew I loved him, but girls fall in love easily. We didn't know much about each other, but if he was planning to stick around, I guess we would.

Before my next words could come out of my mouth, my door flew open and there was a group of people coming in.

"Party over here!" Will's ass just had to be loud. He was the leader of the pack, and then there was Alvin, Stephanie, Sandy, Uncle Johnny, and Mr. Jefferson.

What was Mr. Jefferson doing here—especially without Sade? Before I could ask him where she was, Sade came in on her daddy's shoulders. "Yeah, Mama, you woke up. Now can we have a party, Daddy? With cake and ice cream?"

I sat up and the whole room told me not to move—like I was going to listen. "Come here, Sade. Don't you look beautiful like always. Why are you wearing a princess crown?"

Dre put her on my bed and mouthed, "It's her birthday."

"It must be because today is your birthday. Did I get that right?"

She smiled ear to ear. "Yes, Mama, it's my birthday, and I knew you were going to wake up today. I told my daddy, didn't I tell you, Daddy?"

She was talking to Mr. Jefferson this time, and he was nodding his head yes while staring at the TV with my daddy.

My daddy looked over at Mr. Jefferson and said, "Larry, you heard about that boy there? He grew up with Savannah. He couldn't pass the NBA physical. They say he is HIV-positive. Cal dropped him from the team when he returned; then he shot himself and lived. He's a vegetable now." I knew who my daddy was talking about, but I couldn't look at the TV screen.

The nurse entered my room with a birthday cake for Sade. I thought Dre might have set it up. "Look at you, Mr. Dre. On top of everything for your daughter, I see."

He was clueless as to where the cake came from and nobody spoke up and took credit for it, so I asked the nurse.

"Did the hospital provide this for my daughter?"

She set the cake down and said, "No, the new candy striper that was in here when you woke up did. She was leaving and asked me to drop it off."

I hadn't seen that lady since I opened my eyes. That was very sweet of her to get Sade a cake. I know they aren't paid for what they do. They're more like hospital volunteers.

"Well, tell her we said thank you." My daddy had spoken up since I hadn't.

"I will, sir. She'll be in here with you tonight, Savannah. She has sat with you every night since your second week here. You were her first patient and only patient. She said there was just something about you."

The nurse smiled and exited the room. Sandy stood up and started singing happy birthday to Sade, and everybody joined in.

"Dre, why don't you take little Miss Sade to the cafeteria so we can get some plates."

I knew this was coming. Sandy doesn't bite her tongue. I'm surprised she waited for those two to leave the room.

"Start talking. I've waited three months for you to wake your ass up."

I laughed, and then rubbed my head. I hadn't realized I was bald until that very second. I had worn a short cut before, so I wasn't worried about my appearance.

"First thing first is to fight this cancer and beat it, and then I need to set up a room for Sade at my house. I am not taking her from you. I just want to be a part of the family, Mr. Jefferson."

Stephanie stepped up. "And Dre? That's a good-ass man. If you don't want him, *I'll* take him."

Sandy and Will nodded their heads in agreement, and Alvin hit Will in the stomach.

"I think it's time for us to date and start where we left off . . . That's only if he is willing."

Memphis stood up and stretched. "Dating would be a good idea since y'all live together now. Don't look at me like that. Look at your daddy. He works at the restaurant with the Jeffersons. He said you're holding up the marriage. Me and Daddy already gave him the okay to have you."

What was wrong with these people around me? Had *everybody* suffered brain damage? "Y'all do understand before all of this I had only spent *one* week with him, right?" Everybody nodded their heads in unison, even Mr. Jefferson.

"There will not be any wedding bells soon, I can promise you that. But I do love him." The door flew open, and Dre walked in with plates, spoons, and napkins, and Sade handed me flowers.

"I love you too, Savannah, and when I get you home, your last name will be Burns like mine and Sade's, ain't that right, baby?"

Sade hurried up and answered, "Yes."

My doctor stuck his head in the room and asked if we could wrap it up in an hour because they needed to get me prepared for tomorrow's surgery.

"Calm down, tiger, they taking it out. It's your lucky day. It hasn't spread or anything, but as a precaution, it's got to go."

Will just made it sound like losing my baby-making organs was a walk in the park. Yes, I've always wanted a hysterectomy and tried to get one many times, but with a man who loves kids like Dre, what if he wants more?

We ate our cake and wrapped up Sade's hospital party. I hated to see everyone leave, but they all promised to be in the room waiting on me when I got out of surgery.

I turned on the news and watched Ant's tragic story in disgust. I knew I had something, or should I say, *everything,* to do with it, but he didn't have to try to take his life. He had made matters a lot worse. He has a child. Wouldn't you think about your child first? Yes, I gave Sade away, and it was a good thing that I did. I wasn't ready for her, and I still wasn't. It was in her best interest to be with the Jeffersons.

There were two soft knocks on my door, and then it opened. It was the nurse who brought

Sade the cake. "Thank you so much for the cake. It really made her day."

She pulled a chair up to my bed and grabbed my hands. "You are welcome. She's a doll. I met her two weeks ago with her father. They were asleep next to you. When I woke her up, she introduced herself to me, and the introduction included her birthday. Her daddy said she got the mouth from you." She smiled, and then asked me, "Are you ready for your big day tomorrow?"

She was a beautiful, bright-skinned African American woman with dimples and tight eyes to match. She was Creole, I assumed, because she had a heavy Louisianan accent.

"As ready as I will ever be, I guess."

She patted my hand some more and stood up. "Well, I guess there is no need for me to stay the night with you. You're awake now. I will check on you tomorrow night before I head back home. This hospital isn't my cup of tea. It's time to head back South."

I didn't know this woman at all, but I didn't want to be alone in this room. I wouldn't sleep. "The doctor is checking on me shortly but once he leaves, I would like you to stay one more night with me, if you don't mind. I can't stand hospitals, I never have."

She agreed to return, and then left. With everything going on, I never thought about what happened to Keisha after our meeting at the job, and I wondered if I still had a job. I called Stephanie to ask her.

"Yes, Savannah, you still have your job. Mr. Williams has your back. He pressed trespassing charges against Keisha to go along with her attempted murder charge, and he even pressed charges on Erika for lying on her job application about her background, which is a federal offense. You are loved by that company, girl, so stop tripping. We are going to get this cancer out of you and get you back in the office soon. I love you and get you some rest."

The next call I made was to my house. I needed to speak with Dre.

"Hello," he answered on the first ring. "How are you feeling, baby? Is something wrong?"

I had to answer his question, "Yes, Dre, there are a lot of things wrong. You don't know me, Dre. I mean, you don't know the real me, and how could you because I don't know her, either. Look at everything I have done to you in the last five years. I hid your child from you, Dre. I played childish games that messed up a lot of people's lives. I'm not shit. Why would you want to waste your time trying to deal with a woman like me? There is a good girl out there for you, a woman who wouldn't play mind games. Why me, Dre? Is it because of Sade? Huh? Tell me the truth. I can handle anything after facing death twice."

He took a deep breath. "Savannah, you don't think that I haven't asked myself that question a thousand times? When I saw you in Vegas with that nigga, then watched you go to a hotel with another nigga for lunch, followed by you taking another nigga to your beach house to fuck you the same night, you think that shit didn't cross my mind? The first question I asked myself was why I was chasing down a ho."

He was silent for a moment, and then continued. "My goal then became to get Sade and bounce, leave you to fucking any nigga you wanted to. Then, I broke into your place after the little orgy you had and watched the videos that you labeled *Revenge*. My boy sent me you and Stephanie's phone taps plotting shit. I knew they had to have fucked you over badly for you to go that far. Baby, that week we spent together was magical. I saw fireworks and every damn thing. The Sunday I went home to be with Tasha and my son, I couldn't get you off my mind. I gave Tasha the best dick I had ever given her because I was pretending like I was fucking you, like I was deep in you.

"Yes, beautiful, I used you to buy me some time with the police, but that was so I could end shit with Tasha. My mama has full custody of my son now, and when we get married, he's coming to stay with us. Tasha turned snitch and was helping the police the whole time. I knew she was helping them, but I couldn't tell anybody, because if I did, they would know I knew they were coming. If I wouldn't have spent the night with you, I would have gotten arrested at the club that night.

"Baby, I do right by people. I'm not violent at all. I just like money and found an easier way to get it besides working an eight to five. With the help of my boys, I've made well over a million dollars in three years. When you making money like that, you let the police get you on the small shit so you can get away with the big shit. Baby, we straight: you, Andre Jr., Sade, and me. I love you, and you will be my wife. If you want to take it slow and get to know each other, that's cool too, but I ain't going nowhere. I don't want to make it work for Sade. I want it to work for us, baby. It's Kismet."

Tears were pouring from my eyes. The doctors were ready for me. I put the phone back to my ear and told Dre that I loved him and went for more exams.

***

When I woke up after my surgery, my room was packed with familiar faces, balloons, and flowers. Physically, I felt empty, like I was missing something, but emotionally, I felt reborn. "Dre, baby, come here."

I couldn't see him, but I knew he was nearby. For the last five years he hadn't left my side, so why would he now? When he came within arm's reach, I grabbed him and kissed his lips. The whole room commented, but the only comment that caught my full attention was Sade's.

"Mama just woke up and didn't brush her teeth, and she kissing Daddy—Yuck!" She was snitching on me to Mrs. Jefferson, who joined the crew today.

"Now that Savannah is fully woke, y'all gather around and hold hands." Mrs. Jefferson said a prayer of thanks and asked for new beginnings for everyone in the room. When she was done, I felt the need to break the silence that followed the prayer.

"I sure could do for some peach cobbler when I get out of here."

She smiled and rubbed my shoulders. "You will get plenty of that each week at our family dinners on Sundays. Your daddy and fiancé love them, don't y'all? As soon as your daddy gets out of church, he ready to eat." Everyone laughed.

"Savannah, the doctors said they think they got it all. You will be here another two weeks, and then you can come home. I can't wait so you can get a pool man over there; then we can have a pool party."

That was typical of Memphis, ready to swim. That comment made me remember how close we were before I started messing with Kim. Memphis was my best friend, and hopefully, we could get that back.

I wasn't trying to be rude, but I was tired and really felt like going to sleep. I told everyone I loved them and fell asleep before the last person had left my room.

I woke up to the theme music of one of those late-night talk shows and wasn't surprised to see the nurse standing over me.

"Everything is looking good, Savannah. You beat this one like a champ." She had come to see me, and I still didn't know her name.

"It feels like I was in a fight too. I'm sorry, I never caught your name."

There was a brief hesitation, and then she said, "Everybody calls me Peaches, baby. I got the nickname from one too many cobblers. Now that you're done with this, what are your next plans?"

I was glad that I actually had a plan to share. "I'm going to raise my daughter and my future stepson and give this family thing a real shot. It's never been in me to be somebody's wife or someone's mother. I lived for me, and that didn't work. So, I'm going to try something new and live for them."

Peaches looked me dead in the eyes. "That's right, baby, take care of your family. It won't work if the woman is weak and selfish. You got to put what you want to the side and get what is best for you all. You're young, so it's not too late to get back in them babies' lives the way you should be. Once you leave them, a lot of times you don't get to come back, even when you beg to."

It was like a light switch the way it turned on. I could see things clearer than I had before. Missing puzzle pieces were adding up and all the hurt and anger I had just decided to let go came speeding back. It was the dimples like Sade's and peach cobbler that gave her ass away.

"So, what made you decide to bring your ass back, Mama?"

To be continued . . .